To Greg —

with many

thanks

W. A. C.

Aug. 3,
1995

DYING
IN THE
POST-WAR
WORLD

Books by MAX ALLAN COLLINS

THE MEMOIRS OF NATHAN HELLER
True Detective
True Crime
The Million-Dollar Wound
Neon Mirage
Stolen Away
Dying in the Post-War World

NOLAN AND JON NOVELS
Bait Money
Blood Money
Fly Paper
Hush Money
Hard Cash
Scratch Fever
Spree

QUARRY NOVELS
The Broker (retitled: Quarry)
The Broker's Wife (retitled: Quarry's List)
The Dealer (retitled: Quarry's Deal)
The Slasher (retitled: Quarry's Cut)
Primary Target

MALLORY NOVELS
No Cure for Death
The Baby Blue Rip-Off
Kill Your Darlings
A Shroud for Aquarius
Nice Weekend for a Murder

ELIOT NESS NOVELS
The Dark City
Butcher's Dozen
Bullet Proof

NOVELS
Midnight Haul
Dick Tracy (film novelization)
Dick Tracy Goes to War

CRITICAL STUDIES
One Lonely Knight: Mickey Spillane's Mike Hammer (with James Traylor)
The Best of Crime and Detective TV (with John Javna)

EDITOR
Tomorrow I die (Mickey Spillane short-story collection)
Mike Hammer: The Comic Strip (two volumes)
Dick Tracy: The Secret Files (with Martin H. Greenberg)
The Dick Tracy Casebook (with Dick Locher)

MAX ALLAN COLLINS

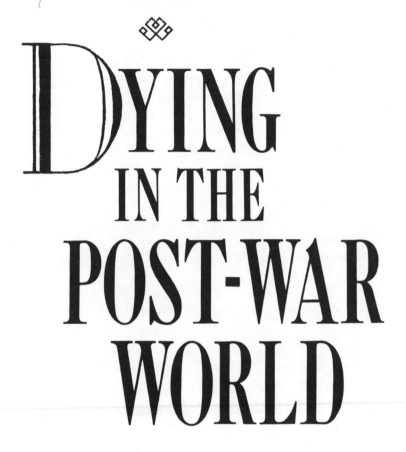

DYING
IN THE
POST-WAR
WORLD

A Nathan Heller Casebook

A FOUL PLAY PRESS BOOK
THE COUNTRYMAN PRESS
Woodstock, Vermont

Copyright © 1984, 1986, 1987, 1988, 1990, and 1991 by Max Allan Collins.

"Foreword," copyright © 1991 by Edward Gorman.

Dying in the Post-War World (collection), copyright © 1991 by Max Allan Collins.

First Edition

10 9 8 7 6 5 4 3 2 1

Library of Congress Cataloging-in-Publication Data

Collins, Max Allan.
 Dying in the post-war world : a Nathan Heller casebook / Max Allan Collins. — 1st ed.
   p. cm.
 "A Foul Play Press book."
 ISBN 0-88150-210-3
 1. Heller, Nathan (Fictitious character)—Fiction. 2. Detective and mystery stories, American. I. Title
PS3553.04753D9 1991   91-22498
813'.54—dc20   CIP

Printed in the United States of America
Text design by Ruth Kolbert

A Foul Play Press Book
The Countryman Press, Inc.
Woodstock, Vermont

F O R
Louis Wilder
who defines grace under pressure

Although the historical events in these stories are portrayed more or less accurately (as much as the passage of time, and contradictory source material, will allow), fact, speculation, and fiction are freely mixed here; historical personages exist side by side with composite characters and wholly fictional ones—all of whom act and speak at the author's whim.

CONTENTS

FOREWORD
Raising Heller

He was old now, in his eighties, and he had survived the pulps and had then survived the early paperback originals, but he was done now, he would survive nothing more, and he knew it. He wrote to me: "I never found a hero the public liked enough to visit more than a couple of times. It's a curse when your hero starts having a life of his own, but it's a bigger curse when your hero never has any life at all." This was our next to last letter. A dour month later, chill and rainy night, he died in his armchair watching TV.

He left a lot of books behind, and some very good ones indeed, but as he said he'd never found "a hero the public liked enough to visit more than a couple of times."

Sometimes you don't know which curse is worse, having a series character the public won't let you give up (à la Arthur Conan Doyle and Sherlock Holmes) or having a series character nobody cares about.

Max Allan Collins (Al to his friends) wrote three series before he came to Nathan Heller, his Chicago private eye of the thirties, forties, and fifties, and while Nolan the thief and Mallory the mystery writer and Quarry the hit man are men the public has happily visited more than a few times, it was Nate Heller who brought Al his first major audience.

I have an explanation for this. I think the private-eye works better in the past and the future ("Bladerunner," say) than he does in the present.

In the present, he's not quite believable. In a world of SWAT-teams, industrial spies, Secret Service men and narcs—not to mention mercenaries and terrorists—the private eye seems an awfully romantic and slightly irrelevant conceit. (I say this, of course, as someone who writes modern day private eye stories himself.)

Nathan Heller lives in a world of Chesterfields, Sen-Sen, cigarette girls, cars with running boards, hats with snap-brims, and women with pasts. It is the ultimate *noir* world: the nighttime streets shine lonely with spring rain, the sound of footsteps haunts the dark brick alleys of midtown, and more than one hooker goes to bed with a john in her arms and a farm-girl's Hail Mary on her lips.

And then Al imposes himself on all this—or that part of himself that is also Nate Heller. Where most of us go in for long stretches of unabashed autobiography in our novels, Al remains sly as ever. You get him—or the "him" I perceive anyway—in bits and pieces of Heller's conversations and actions. Al is every bit as charming as Heller—my wife would say even more so—but he's not quite as dark. Al tends to redeem everything with his humor. I found this out when I went through a medical scare a few years ago. Al phoned every night for two weeks and forced me to laugh. I can't ever recall a more important kindness. Heller would no doubt be sympathetic to my fears but the most I would get from him is a manly pat on the back and a pack of smokes. No jokes at all.

With the possible exception of *Butcher's Dozen,* a Collins novel in the Eliot Ness series, the Hellers represent Al's best writing. The subject matter demands that Al use the entire symphony to achieve his effects. (Nolan is a jazz trio; Mallory a rock and roll garage band; and Quarry a very dark country western group, say Johnny Cash back in the fifties when he was singing "Mystery Train" even better than Elvis.) With the founding of Las Vegas, World War II, and the Capone wars as just a few of his backdrops and themes, Al knew he had to write better than he ever had before. And he did. And he keeps on doing it.

The funny thing about this collection is that five years ago it couldn't have existed. Why? Well, first of all because the book's one smashing original, "Dying in the Post-War World," hadn't been written then. But more important, in those days Al still didn't think he was very good at short stories.

This wasn't necessarily undue modesty. A) He hadn't written many short stories. B) Many novelists, even/especially quite famous ones, write execrable shorter work. And C) He wasn't sure anybody would want his short fiction even if he could overcome his doubts and write some of the stuff.

Well, he soon learned better. Editors (me included) love his short fiction and demand for it keeps increasing. Just the other day, Joe Lansdale said he plans to invite Collins into the next anthology he edits: "I read a couple of his stories and he's damn good."

You'll like these stories. They're tough, wry, sly, sexy, angry, witty, bitchy, violent, colorful, introspective and just plain good.

And God knows you'll like Nate Heller. He's just the kind of guy you'll want to visit more than a couple of times. Lots more. I promise.

—ED GORMAN

DYING IN THE POST-WAR WORLD

L IFE WAS PRETTY MUCH PERFECT. I had a brand-new brown-brick G.I. Bill bungalow in quietly suburban Lincolnwood; Peggy, my wife since December of last year, was ripely pregnant; I'd bribed a North Side car dealer into getting one of the first new Plymouths; and I'd just moved the A-1 Detective Agency into the prestigious old Rookery Building in the Loop.

True, business was a little slow—a good share of A-1's trade, over the years, has been divorce work, and nobody was getting divorced right now. It was July of 1947, and former soldiers and their blushing brides were still fucking, not fighting, but that would come. I was patient. In the meantime, there were plenty of credit checks to run. People were spending dough, chasing after their post-war dreams.

Sunlight was filtering in through the sheer curtains of our little bedroom, teasing my beautiful wife into wakefulness. I was already up—it was a quarter to eight, and I tried to be in to work by nine (when you're the boss, punctuality is optional). I was standing near the bed, snugging my tie, when Peg looked up at me through slits.

"I put the coffee on," I said. "I can scramble you some eggs, if you like. Fancier than that, you're your own."

"What time is it?" She sat up; the covers slid down the slope of her tummy. Her swollen breasts poked at the gathered top of her nightgown.

I told her the time, even though a clock was on the nightstand nearby.

She swallowed thickly. Blinked. Peg's skin was pale, translucent; a faint trail of freckles decorated a pert nose. Her eyebrows were thick, her eyes big and violet. Without make-up, her dark brown curly locks a mess, seven months pregnant, first thing in the morning, she was gorgeous.

She, of course, didn't think so. She had told me repeatedly, for the last two months—when her pregnancy had begun to make itself blatantly obvious—that she looked hideous and bloated. Less than ten years ago, she'd been an artist's model; just a year ago, she'd been a smartly dressed young business-woman. Now, she was a pregnant housewife, and not a happy one.

That was why I'd been making breakfast for the last several weeks.

Out in the hall, the phone rang.

"I'll get it," I said.

She nodded; she was sitting on the bed, easing her swollen feet into pink slippers, a task she was approaching with the care and precision of a bomb-squad guy removing a detonator.

I got it on the third ring. "This is Heller," I said.

"Nate . . . this is Bob."

I didn't recognize the voice, but I recognized the tone: desperation, with some despair mixed in.

"Bob . . . ?"

"Bob Keenan," the tremulous voice said.

"Oh! Bob." And I immediately wondered why Bob Keenan,

who just a passing acquaintance, would be calling me at home, first thing in the morning. Keenan was a friend and client of an attorney I did work for, and I'd had lunch with both of them, at Binyon's, around the corner from my old office on Van Buren, perhaps four times over the past six months. That was the extent of it.

"I hate to bother you at home . . . but something . . . something *awful's* happened. You're the only person I could think of who can help me. Can you come, straight-away?"

"Bob, do you want to talk about this?"

"Not on the phone! Come right away. Please?"

That last word was a tortured cry for help.

I couldn't turn him down. Whatever was up, this guy was hurting. Besides which, Keenan was well off—he was one of the top administrators at the Office of Price Administration. So there might be some dough in it.

"Sure," I said. "I'll be right there."

He gave me the address (of his home), and I wrote it down and hung up; went out in the kitchen, where Peg sat in her white terry cloth bathrobe, staring over her black coffee.

"Can you fix yourself something, honey?" I asked. "I'm going to have to skip breakfast."

Peg looked at me hollow-eyed.

"I want a divorce," she said.

I swallowed. "Well, maybe I do have time to fix you a little breakfast."

She looked at me hard. "I'm not kidding, Nate. I want a divorce."

I nodded. Sighed, and said, "We'll talk about it later."

She looked away. Sipped her coffee. "Let's do that," she said.

I slipped on my suitcoat and went out into the bright, sunny day. Birds were chirping. From down the street came the gentle whir of a lawn mower. It would be hot later, but right now it was pleasant, even a little cool.

The dark blue Plymouth was at the curb and I went to it. Well, maybe this wasn't all bad: maybe this meant A-1's business would be picking up, now that divorce had finally come home from the war.

2

The house—mansion, really—had once belonged to a guy named Murphy who invented the bed of the same name, one of which I had slept in many a night, back when my office and my apartment were one and the same. But the rectangular cream-color brick building, wearing its jaunty green hat of a roof, had long ago been turned into a two-family dwelling.

Nonetheless, it was an impressive residence, with a sloping lawn and a twin-pillared entrance, just a block from the lake on the far North Side. And the Keenan family had a whole floor to themselves, the first, with seven spacious rooms. Bob Keenan was doing all right, with his OPA position.

Only right now he wasn't doing so good.

He met me at the front door; in shirtsleeves, no tie, his fleshy face long and pale, eyes wide with worry. He was around forty years of age, but something, this morning, had added an immediate extra ten years.

"Thank you, Nate," he said, grasping my hand eagerly, "thank you for coming."

"Sure, Bob," I said.

He ushered me through the nicely but not lavishly furnished apartment like a guy with the flu showing a plumber where the busted toilet was.

"Look in here," he said, and he held out his palm. I entered what was clearly a child's room, a little girl's room. Pink floral wallpaper, a graceful tiny wooden bed, slippers on the rug nearby, sheer feminine curtains, a toy chest on which various dolls sat like sweetly obedient children.

I shrugged. "What . . . ?"

"This is JoAnn's room," he said, as if that explained it.

"Your little girl?"

He nodded. "The younger of my two girls. Jane's with her mother in the kitchen."

The bed was unmade; the window was open. Lake wind whispered in.

"Where's JoAnn, Bob?" I asked.

"Gone," he said. He swallowed thickly. "Look at this."

He walked to the window; pointed to a scrap of paper on the floor. I walked there, knelt. I did not pick up the greasy scrap of foolscap. I didn't have to, to read the crudely printed words there:

Get $20,000 Ready & Waite for Word. Do Not
Notify FBI or Police. Bills in 5's and 10's. Burn this
for her safty!

I stood and sucked in some air; hands on hips, I looked into Bob Keenan's wide, red, desperate eyes and said, "You haven't called the cops?"

"No. Or the FBI. I called you."

Sounding more irritable than I meant to, I said, "For Christ's sake, why?"

"The note said no police. I needed help. I may need an intermediary. I sure as hell need somebody who knows his way around this kind of thing."

I gestured with open, raised palms, like a mime making a

wall. "Don't touch anything. Have you touched anything?"

"No. Not even the note."

"Good. Good." I put my hand on his shoulder. "Now, just take it easy, Bob. Let's go sit in the living room."

I walked him in there, hand never leaving his shoulder.

"Okay," I said gently, "why exactly did you call *me*?"

He was next to me on the couch, sitting slumped, staring downward, legs apart, hands clasped. He was a big man—not fat: big.

He shrugged. "I knew you worked on the Lindbergh case."

Yeah, and hadn't *that* worked out swell.

"I was a cop, then," I said. "I was the liaison between the Chicago p.d. and the New Jersey authorities. And that was a long time ago."

"Well, Ken mentioned it once."

"Did you call Ken before you called me? Did he suggest you call me?"

Ken was the attorney who was our mutual friend and business associate.

"No. Nate . . . to be quite frank, I called you because, well . . . you're supposed to be connected."

I sighed. "I've had dealings with the Outfit from time to time, but I'm no gangster, Bob, and even if I was . . ."

"I didn't mean that! If you were a gangster, do you think I would have called you?"

"I'm not understanding this, Bob."

His wife, Norma, entered the room tentatively; she was a pretty, petite woman in a floral print dress that was like a darker version of the wallpaper in her little girl's room. Her pleasant features were distorted; there was a wildness in her face. She hadn't cried yet. She was too upset.

I stood. If I'd ever felt more awkward, I couldn't remember when.

"Is everything all right, Bob? Is this your detective friend?"

"Yes. This is Nate Heller."

She came to me and gave me a skull-like smile. "Thank for you coming. Oh, thank you so much for coming. Can you help us?"

"Yes," I said. It was the only thing I could say.

Relief filled her chest and filtered up through her face; but her eyes remained wild.

"Please go sit with Jane," Bob said, patting her arm. He looked at me as if an explanation were necessary. "Jane and her little sister are so very close. She and JoAnn are only two years apart."

I nodded, and the wife went hurriedly away, as if rushing to make sure Jane was still there.

We sat back down.

"I know you've had dealings with the mob," Keenan said. "The problem is . . . so have I. Or actually, the problem is, I haven't."

"Pardon?"

He sighed and shook his head. "I only moved here six months ago. I'd been second-in-command in the New York office. In Albany."

"Of the OPA, you mean?"

"Yes," he said, nodding. "I guess I don't have to tell you the pressures a person in my position is under. We're in charge of everything from building and industrial materials to meat to gasoline to . . . well. Anyway. I didn't play ball with the mobsters out there. There were threats against me, against my family, but I didn't take their money. I asked for a transfer. I was sent here."

Chicago? That was a hell of a place to hide from mobsters.

He read the thought in my face.

"I know," he said, raising an eyebrow, "but I wasn't given

a choice in the matter. Oddly, none of that type of people have contacted me here. But then, things are winding down . . . rationing's all but a thing of the past." He laughed mirthlessly. "That's the irony. The sad goddamn irony."

"What is?"

He was shaking his head. "The announcement will be made later this week: the OPA is out of business. They're shutting us down. I'm moving over to a Department of Agriculture position."

"I see." I let out another sigh; it was that kind of situation. "So, because the note said not to notify the authorities, and because you've had threats from gangsters before, you called me in."

I had my hands on my knees; he placed his hand over my nearest one, and squeezed. It was an earnest gesture, and embarrassed the hell out of me.

"You've got to help us," he said.

"I will. I will. I'll be glad to serve as an intermediary, and I'll be glad to advise you and do whatever you think will be useful."

"Thank God," he said.

"But first we call the cops."

"What . . . ?"

"Are you a gambling man, Bob?"

"Well, yes, I suppose, in a small way, but not with my daughter's *life*, for God's sake!"

"I know what the odds are in a case like this. In a case like this, children are recovered unharmed more frequently when the police and FBI are brought in."

"But the note said . . ."

"How old is JoAnn?"

"She's six."

"That's old enough for her to be able to describe her

kidnappers. That's old enough for her to pick them out of a line-up."

"I don't understand what you're saying."

"Bob." And now I reached over and clasped his hand. He looked at me with haunted, watery eyes. "Kidnapping's a federal offense, Bob. It's a capital crime."

He swallowed. "Then they'll probably kill her, won't they? If she isn't dead already."

"Your chances are better with the authorities in on it. We'll work it from both ends: negotiate with the kidnappers, even as the cops are beating the bushes trying to find the bastards. And JoAnn."

"If she's not already dead," he said.

I just looked at him. Then I nodded.

He began to weep.

I patted his back, gently. There there. There there.

―――――
3
―――――

The first cop to arrive was Detective Kruger from Summerdale District Station; he was a stocky man in a rumpled suit with an equally rumpled face. His was the naturally mournful countenance of a hound. He looked a little more mournful than usual as he glanced around the child's bedroom.

Keenan was tagging along, pointing things out. "That window," Keenan said, "I only had it open maybe five inches, last night, to let in the breeze. But now it's wide open."

Kruger nodded, taking it all in.

"And the bed-clothes—JoAnn would never fold them back neatly like that."

Kruger looked at Keenan with eyes that were sharp in the folds of his face. "You heard nothin' unusual last night?"

Keenan flinched, almost as if embarrassed. "Well . . . my wife did."

"Could I speak to her?"

"Not just yet. Not just yet."

"Bob," I said, prompting him, trying not to intrude on Kruger but wanting to be of help, "what did Norma hear?"

"She heard the neighbor's dog barking—sometime after midnight. She sat up in bed, wide awake, thought she heard JoAnn's voice. Went to JoAnn's door, listened, didn't hear anything . . . and went back to bed."

Kruger nodded somberly.

"Please don't ask her about it," Keenan said. "She's blaming herself."

We all knew that was foolish of her; but we all also knew there was nothing to be done about it.

The Scientific Crime Detection Laboratory team arrived, as did the photographer attached to Homicide, and soon the place was swarming with suits and ties. Kruger, who I knew a little, which was why I'd asked for him specifically when I called the Summerdale station, buttonholed me.

"Look, Heller," he said pleasantly, brushing something off the shoulder of my suitcoat. "I know you're a good man, but there's people on the force who think you smell."

A long time ago, I had testified against a couple of crooked cops—crooked even by Chicago standards. By my standards, even. But cops, like crooks, weren't supposed to rat each other out; and even fifteen years later that put me on a lot of shit lists.

"I'll try to stay downwind," I said.

"Good idea. When the feds show, they're not going to relish havin' a private eye on the scene, either."

"I'm only here because Bob Keenan wants me."

"I think he needs you here," Kruger said, nodding, "for his peace of mind. Just stay on the sidelines."

I nodded back.

Kruger had turned to move on, when as an afterthought he looked back and said, "Hey, uh—sorry about your pal Drury. That's a goddamn shame."

I'd worked with Bill Drury on the pickpocket detail back in the early thirties; he was that rare Chicago animal: an honest cop. He also had an obsessive hatred for the Outfit which had gotten him in trouble. He was currently on suspension.

"Let that be a lesson to you," I said cheerfully. "That's what happens to cops who do their jobs."

Kruger shrugged and shambled off, to oversee the forensic boys.

The day was a long one. The FBI arrived in all their officious glory; but they were efficient, putting a tape recorder on the phone in case a ransom call should come in. Reporters got wind of the kidnapping, but outside the boys in blue roped off the area and were keeping them out for now—a crime lab team was making plaster impressions of footprints and probable ladder indentations under the bedroom window. A radio station crew was allowed to come in so Bob could record pleas to the kidnappers ("She's just a little girl . . . please don't hurt her . . . she was only wearing her pajamas, so wrap a blanket around her, please"). Beyond the fingerprinting and photos, the only real policework I witnessed was a brief interrogation of the maid of the family upstairs; a colored girl named Leona, she reported hearing JoAnn say, "I'm sleepy," around half past midnight. Leona's room was directly above the girl's.

Kruger came over and sat on the couch next to me, around lunch time. "Want to grab a bite somewhere, Heller?"

"Sure."

He drove me to a corner café four blocks away and we sat

at the counter. "We found a ladder," he said. "In a back yard a few houses to the south of Keenan's."

"Yeah? Does it match the indentations in the ground?"

Kruger nodded.

"Any scratches on the bricks near the window?"

Kruger nodded again. "Matches those, too. Ladder was a little short."

The first floor window was seven and a half feet off the ground; the basement windows of the building were mostly exposed, in typical Chicago fashion.

"Funny thing," Kruger said. "Ladder had a broken rung."

"A broken rung? Jesus. Just like . . ." I cut myself off.

"Like the Lindbergh case," Kruger said. "You worked that, didn't you?"

"Yeah."

"They killed that kid, didn't they?"

"That's the story."

"This one's dead, too, isn't she?"

The waitress came and poured us coffee.

"Probably," I said.

"Keenan thinks maybe the Outfit's behind this," Kruger said.

"I know he does."

"What do you think, Heller?"

I laughed humorlessly. "Not in a million years. This is an amateur, and a stupid one."

"Oh?"

"Who else would risk the hot seat for twenty grand?"

He considered that briefly. "You know, Heller—Keenan's made some unpopular decisions on the OPA board."

"Not unpopular enough to warrant something like this."

"I suppose." He was sugaring his coffee—overdoing it, now that sugar wasn't so scarce. His hound-dog face studied the swirling coffee as his spoon churned it up. "How do you haul a kid out of her room in the middle of the night without causing a stir?"

"I can think of two ways."

"Yeah?"

"It was somebody who knew her, and she went willingly, trustingly."

"Yeah."

"Or," I said, "they killed her in bed, and carried her out like a sack of sugar."

Kruger swallowed thickly; then he raised his coffee and sipped. "Yeah," he said.

4

I left Kruger at the counter where he was working on a big slice of apple pie, and used a pay phone to call home.

"Nate," Peg said, before I'd had a chance to say anything, "don't you know that fellow Keenan? Robert Keenan?"

"Yes," I said.

"I just heard him on the radio," she said. Her voice sounded both urgent and upset. "His daughter . . ."

"I know," I said. "Bob Keenan is who called me this morning. He called me before he called the police."

There was a pause. Then: "Are you working on the case?"

"Yes. Sort of. The cops and the FBI, it's their baby." Poor choice of words. I moved ahead quickly: "But Bob wants me around. In case an intermediary is needed or something."

"Nate, you've got to help him. You've got to help him get his little girl back."

This morning was forgotten. No talk of divorce now. Just a pregnant mother frightened by the radio, wanting some reassurance from her man. Wanting him to tell her that this glorious post-war world really was a wonderful, safe place to bring a child into.

"I'll try, Peg. I'll try. Don't wait supper for me."

That afternoon, a pair of plainclothes men gave Kruger a sobering report. They stayed out of Keenan's earshot, but Kruger didn't seem to mind my eavesdropping.

They—and several dozen more plainclothes dicks— had been combing the neighborhood, talking to neighbors and specifically to the janitors of the many apartment buildings in the area. One of these janitors had found something disturbing in his basement laundry room.

"Blood smears in a laundry tub," a thin young detective told Kruger.

"And a storage locker that had been broken into," his older, but just as skinny partner said. "Some shopping bags scattered around—and some rags that were stained, too. Reddish-brown stains."

Kruger stared at the floor. "Let's get a forensic team over there."

The detectives nodded, and went off to do that.

Mrs. Keenan and ten-year-old Jane were upstairs, at the neighbors, through all of this; but Bob stayed at the phone, waiting for it to ring. It didn't.

I stayed pretty close to him, though I circulated from time to time, picking up on what the detectives were saying. The mood was grim. I drank a lot of coffee, till I started feeling jumpy, then backed off.

Late afternoon, Kruger caught my eye and I went over to him.

"That basement with the laundry tubs," he said quietly. "In

one of the drains, there were traces of blood, chips of bone, fragments of flesh, little clumps of hair."

"Oh God."

"I'm advising Chief of Detectives Storm to send teams out looking."

"Looking for what?"

"What do you think?"

"God."

"Heller, I want to get started right now. I can use you. Give Keenan some excuse."

I went over to Bob, who sat on the edge of a straightback chair by the phone stand. His glazed eyes were fixed on the phone.

"I'm going to run home for supper," I told him. "Little woman's in the family way, you know, and I got to check in with her or get in dutch. Can you hold down the fort?"

"Sure, Nate. Sure. You'll come back, though?"

I patted his shoulder. "I'll come right back."

Kruger and I paired up; half a dozen other teams, made up of plainclothes and uniformed men already at the scene, went out into the field as well. More were on the way. We were to look under every porch, behind every bush, in every basement, in every coal bin, trash can, any possible hiding place where a little body—or what was left of one—might be stowed.

"We'll check the sewers, too," Kruger said, as we walked down the sidewalk. It was dusk now; the streetlamps had just come on. Coolness off the lake helped you forget it was July. The city seemed washed in gray-blue, but night hadn't stolen away the clarity of day.

I kept lifting manhole covers and Kruger would cast the beam of his flashlight down inside, but we saw nothing but muck.

"Let's not forget the catch basins," I said.

"Good point."

We began checking those as well, and in the passageway between two brick apartment buildings directly across from the building that housed that bloody laundry tub, the circular iron catch-basin lid—like a manhole cover, but smaller—looked loose.

"Somebody opened that recently," Kruger said. His voice was quiet but the words were ominous in the stillness of the darkening night.

"We need something to pry it up a little," I said, kneeling. "Can't get my fingers under it."

"Here," Kruger said. He plucked the badge off the breast pocket of his jacket and, bending down, used the point of the star to pry the lid up to where I could wedge my fingers under it.

I slid the heavy iron cover away, and Kruger tossed the beam of the flashlight into the hole.

A face looked up at us.

A child's face, framed in blonde, muck-dampened/darkened hair.

"It looks like a doll," Kruger said. He sounded out of breath.

"That's no doll," I said, and backed away, knowing I'd done as my wife had requested: I'd found Bob Keenan's little girl.

Part of her, anyway.

5

We fished the little head out of the sewer; how exactly, I'd rather not go into. It involved the handle of a broom we borrowed from the janitor of one of the adjacent buildings.

Afterward, I leaned against the bricks in the alley-like

passageway, my back turned away from what we'd found. Kruger tapped me on the shoulder.

"You all right, Heller?"

Uniformed men were guarding the head, which rested on some newspapers we'd spread out on the cement near the catch basin; they were staring down at it like it was some bizarre artifact of a primitive culture.

"About lost my lunch," I said.

"You're white as an Irishman's ass."

"I'm okay."

Kruger lighted up a cigarette; its amber eye glowed.

"Got another of those?" I asked.

"Sure." He got out a deck of Lucky Strikes. Shook one out for me. I took it hungrily and he thumbed a flame on his Zippo and lit me up. "Never saw you smoke before, Heller."

"Hardly ever do. I used to, overseas. Everybody did, over there."

"I bet. You were on Guadalcanal, I hear."

"Yeah."

"Pretty rough?"

"I thought so till tonight."

He nodded. "I made a call. Keenan's assistant, guy that runs the ration board, he's on his way. To make the I.D. Can't put the father through that shit."

"You're thinking, Kruger," I said, sucking on the cigarette. "You're all right."

He grunted noncommittally and went over to greet various cops, uniform and plainclothes, who were arriving; I stayed off to one side, back to the brick wall, smoking my cigarette.

The janitor we'd borrowed the broom from sought me out. He was a thick-necked, white-haired guy in his early fifties; he wore coveralls over a flannel shirt rolled up at the sleeves.

"So sad," he said. His face was as German as his accent.

"What's on your mind, Pop?"

"I saw something."

"Oh?"

"Maybe is not important."

I called Lt. Kruger over, to let him decide.

"About five this morning," the bull-necked janitor said, "I put out some trash. I see man in brown raincoat walking. His head, it was down, inside his collar, like it was cold outside, only it was not cold and not raining, either. He carry shopping bag."

Kruger and I exchanged sharp glances.

"Where did you see this man walking, exactly?" Kruger asked the janitor.

The stocky Kraut led us into the street; he pointed diagonally—right at the brick mansion where the Keenans lived. "He cut across that lawn, and walk west."

"What's your name, Pop?" I asked.

"Otto. Otto Bergstrum."

Kruger gave Otto the janitor over to a pair of plainclothes dicks and they escorted him off to Summerdale District station to take a formal statement.

"Could be a break," Kruger said.

"Could be," I said.

Keenan's OPA co-worker, Walter Munsen, a heavy-set fellow in his late forties, was allowed through the wall of blue uniforms to look at the chubby-cheeked head on the spread-out papers. It looked up at him, its sweet face nicked with cuts, its neck a ragged thing. He said, "Sweet Jesus. That's her. That's little JoAnn."

That was good enough for Kruger.

We walked back to the Keenan place. A starless, moonless night had settled on the city, as if God wanted to blot out what man had done. It didn't work. The flashing red lights of squad cars, and the beams of cars belonging to the morbidly curious, fought the darkness. Reporters and neighbors infested the sidewalks in front of the Keenan place. Word of our grim discovery had spread—but not to Keenan himself.

At the front door, Kruger said, "I'd like you to break it to him, Heller."

"Me? Why the hell me?"

"You're his friend. You're who he called. He'll take it better from you."

"Bullshit. There's no 'better' *in* this."

But I did the deed.

We stood in one corner of the living room. Kruger was at my side, but I did the talking. Keenan's wife was still upstairs at the neighbors. I put a hand on his shoulder and said, "It's not good, Bob."

He already knew from my face. Still, he had to say: "Is she dead?" Then he answered his own question: "You've found her, and she's dead."

I nodded.

"Dear Lord. Dear Lord." He dropped to one knee, as if praying; but he wasn't.

I braced his shoulder. He seemed to want to get back on his feet, so I helped him do that.

He stood there with his head hung and said, "Let me tell JoAnn's mother myself."

"Bob—there's more."

"More? How can there be more?"

"I said it was bad. After she was killed, whoever did it disposed of her body by . . ." God! What words were there to say this? How do you cushion a goddamn fucking blow like this?

"Nate? What, Nate?"

"She was dismembered, Bob."

MAX ALLAN COLLINS

"Dismembered . . . ?"

Better me than some reporter. "I found her head in a sewer catch basin about a block from here."

He just looked at me, eyes white all around; shaking his head, trying to make sense of the words.

Then he turned and faced the wall; hands in his pockets.

"Don't tell Norma," he said, finally.

"We have to tell her," Kruger said, as kindly as he could. "She's going to hear soon enough."

He turned and looked at me; his face was streaked with tears. "I mean . . . don't tell her about . . . the . . . dismembering part."

"Somebody's got to tell her," Kruger insisted.

"Call their parish priest," I told Kruger, and he bobbed his dour hound-dog head.

The priest—Father O'Shea of St. Gertrude's church — arrived just as Mrs. Keenan was being ushered back into her apartment. Keenan took his wife by the arm and walked her to the sofa; she was looking at her silent husband's tragic countenance with alarm.

The priest, a little white-haired fellow with Bible and rosary in hand, said, "How strong is your faith, my child?"

Keenan was sitting next to her; he squeezed her hand, and she looked up with clear eyes, but her lips were trembling. "My faith is strong, Father."

The priest paused, trying to find the words. I knew the feeling.

"Is she all right, Father?" Norma Keenan asked. The last vestiges of hope clung to the question.

The priest shook his head no.

"Is . . . is she hurt?"

The priest shook his head no.

Norma Keenan knew what that meant. She stared at nothing for several long moments. Then she looked up again, but the eyes were cloudy now. "Did they . . ." She began again. "Was she . . . disfigured?"

The priest swallowed.

I said, "No she wasn't, Mrs. Keenan."

Somebody had to have the decency to lie to the woman.

"Thank God," Norma Keenan said. "Thank God."

She began to sob, and her husband hugged her desperately.

6

Just before ten that night, a plainclothes team found JoAnn's left leg in another catch basin. Less than half an hour later, the same team checked a manhole nearby and found her right leg in a shopping bag.

Not long after, the torso turned up—in a sewer gutter, bundled in a fifty-pound cloth sugar bag.

Word of these discoveries rocketed back to the Keenan apartment, which had begun to fill with mucky-mucks—the Police Commissioner, the Chief of Detectives and his Deputy Chief, the head of the homicide detail, the Coroner and, briefly, the Mayor. The State's Attorney and his right-hand investigator Captain Daniel "Tubbo" Gilbert came and stayed.

The big shots showing didn't surprise me, with a headline-bound crime like this. But the arrival of Tubbo Gilbert, who was Outfit all the way, was unsettling—considering Bob Keenan's early concerns about mob involvement.

"Heller," well-dressed Tubbo said amiably, "what rock did you crawl out from under?"

Tubbo looked exactly like his name sounded.

"Excuse me," I said, and brushed past him.

It was time for me to fade.

I went to Bob to say my goodbyes. He was seated on the couch, talking to several FBI men; his wife was upstairs, at the neighbors again, under sedation.

"Nate," Keenan said, standing, patting the air with one hand, his bloodshot eyes beseeching me, "before you go . . . I need a word. Please."

"Sure."

We ducked into the bathroom. He shut the door. My eyes caught a child's yellow rubber duck on the edge of the claw-footed tub.

"I want you to stay on the job," Keenan said.

"Bob, every cop in town is going to be on this case. The last thing you need, or they want, is a private detective in the way."

"Did you see who was out there?"

"A lot of people. Some very good people, mostly."

"That fellow Tubbo Gilbert. I know about him. I was warned about him. They call him 'the Richest Cop in Chicago,' don't they?"

"That's true." And that was saying something, in Chicago. Keenan's eyes narrowed. "He's in with the gangsters."

"He's in with a lot of people, Bob, but . . ."

"I'll write you a check . . ." And he withdrew a checkbook from his pants pocket and knelt at the toilet and began filling a check out, frantically, using the lid as a writing table.

This was as embarrassing as it was sad. "Bob . . . please don't do this . . ."

He stood and handed me a check for one thousand dollars. The ink glistened wetly.

"It's a retainer," he said. "All I want from you is to keep an eye on the case. Keep these Chicago cops honest."

That was a contradiction of terms, but I let it pass.

"Okay," I said, and folded the check up and slipped it in my pocket, smearing the ink probably. I didn't think I'd be keeping it, but the best thing to do right now was just take it.

He pumped my hand and his smile was an awful thing. "Thank you, Nate. God bless you, Nate. Thank you for everything, Nate."

We exited the bathroom and everybody eyed us strangely, as if wondering if we were perverts. Many of these cops didn't like me much, and were glad to see me go.

Outside, several reporters recognized me and called out. I ignored them as I moved toward my parked Plymouth; I hoped I wasn't blocked in. Hal Davis of the *News*, a small man with a big head, bright-eyed and boyish despite his fifty-some years, tagged along.

"You want to make an easy C-note?" Davis said.

"Why I'm fine, Hal. How are you?"

"I hear you were the one that fished the kid's noggin outa the shit soup."

"That's touching, Hal. Sometimes I wonder why you haven't won a Pulitzer yet, with your way with words."

"I want the exclusive interview."

I walked faster. "Fuck you."

"Two C's."

I stopped. "Five."

"Christ! Success has gone to your head, Heller."

"I might do better elsewhere. What's the hell's that all about?"

In the alley behind the Keenan house, some cops were holding reporters back while a crime-scene photographer faced a wooden fence, flashbulbs popping, making little explosions in the night.

"Damned if I know," Davis said, and was right behind me as I moved quickly closer.

The cops kept us back, but we could see it, all right. Written on the fence, in crude red lettering, were the words: "Stop me before I kill more."

"Jesus Christ," Davis said, all banjo-eyed. "Is *that* who did this? The goddamn *lipstick* killer?"

"The lipstick killer," I repeated numbly.

Was that who did this?

7

The Lipstick Killer, as the press had termed him, had hit the headlines for the first time last January.

Mrs. Caroline Williams, an attractive forty-year-old widow with a somewhat shady past, was found nude and dead in bed in her modest North Side apartment. A red skirt and a nylon stocking were tied tightly around the throat of the voluptuous brunette corpse. There had been a struggle, apparently—the room was topsy-turvy. Mrs. Williams had been beaten, her face bruised, battered.

She'd bled to death from a slashed throat, and the bed was soaked red; but she was oddly clean. Underneath the tightly-tied red skirt and nylon, the coroner found an adhesive bandage over the neck wound.

The tub in the bathroom was filled with bloody water and the victim's clothing, as if wash were soaking.

A suspect—an armed robber who was the widow's latest gentleman friend—was promptly cleared. Caroline Williams had been married three times, leaving two divorced husbands and one dead one. Her ex-husbands had unshakable alibis, particularly the latter.

The case faded from the papers, and dead-ended for the cops.

Then just a little over a month ago, a similar crime—apparently, even obviously, committed by the same hand—had rattled the city's cage. Mrs. Williams, who'd gotten around after all, had seemed the victim of a crime of passion. But when Margaret Johnson met a disturbingly similar fate, Chicago knew it had a madman at large.

Margaret Johnson—her friends called her Peggy—was twenty-nine years old and a beauty. A well-liked, church-going small-town girl, she'd just completed three years of war service with the Waves to go to work in the office of a business-machine company in the Loop. She was found nude and dead in her small flat in a North Side residential hotel.

When a hotel maid found her, Miss Johnson was slumped, kneeling, at the bathtub, head over the tub. Her hair was wrapped turban-like in a towel, her pajama top tied loosely around her neck, through which a bread knife had been driven with enough force to go in one side and poke out the other.

She'd also been shot—once in the head, again in the arm. Her palms were cut, presumably from trying to wrest the knife from the killer's hand.

The blood had been washed from the ex-Wave's body. Damp, bloody towels were scattered about the bathroom floor. The outer room of the small apartment was a shambles, bloodstains everywhere. Most significantly, fairly high up on the wall, in letters three to six inches tall, printed in red with the victim's lipstick, were the words:

FOR HEAVENS
SAKE CATCH ME
BEFORE I KILL MORE
I CANNOT CONTROL MYSELF

The cops and the papers called the Lipstick Killer (the nickname was immediate) a "sex maniac," though neither woman had been raped. The certainty of the police in that characterization made me suspicious that something meaningful had been withheld.

I had asked Lt. Bill Drury, who before his suspension had worked the case out of Town Hall Station, and he said semen had been found on the floor in both apartments, near the windows that had apparently given the killer entry in either flat.

What we had here was a guy who needed one hell of a visual aid to jack off.

What these two slain women had in common with the poor butchered little JoAnn Keenan, I wasn't sure, other than violent death at the hands of a madman with something sharp; the body parts of the child were largely drained of blood. That was about it.

But the lipstick message on that alley fence—even down to the child-like lettering—would serve to fuel the fires of this investigation even further. The papers had already been calling the Lipstick Killer "Chicago's Jack the Ripper." With the slaying of the kidnapped girl, the city would undoubtedly go off the deep end.

"The papers have been riding the cops for months," I told Peg that night, as we cuddled in bed; she was trembling in the hollow of my arm. "Calling them Keystone Kops, ridiculing the ineffectiveness of their crime lab work. And their failure to nab the Lipstick Killer has been a club the papers've beat 'em with."

"You sound like you think that's unfair," Peg said.

"I do, actually. A lunatic can be a lot harder to catch than a career criminal. And this guy's M.O. is all over the map."

"M.O.?"

"The way he does his crimes, the kind of crimes he does. Even the two women he killed, there are significant differences. The second was shot, and that, despite the knife through the throat, was the cause of death. Is it okay if I talk about this?"

She nodded. She was a tough cookie.

"Anyway," I went on, "the guy hasn't left a single workable fingerprint."

"Cleans up after himself," she said.

"Half fetish," I said, "half cautious."

"Completely nuts."

"Completely nuts," I agreed. I smiled at her. It was dark in the bedroom, but I could see her sweet face, staring into nothing.

Quietly, she said, "You told your friend Bob Keenan that you'd stay on the job."

"Yeah. I was just pacifying him."

"You *should* stay on it."

"I don't know if I can. The cops, hell the feds, they're not exactly going to line up for my help."

"Since when does that kind of thing stop you? Keep on it. You've got to find this fiend." She took my hand and placed it on her full tummy. "Got to."

"Sure, Peg. Sure."

I gave her tummy the same sort of "there there" pat I'd given Bob Keenan's shoulder. And I felt a strange, sick gratefulness to the Lipstick Killer, suddenly: the day had begun with my wife asking for a divorce.

It had ended with me holding her, comforting her.

In this glorious post-war world, I'd take what I could get.

8

Two days later, I was treating my friend Bill Drury to lunch in the bustling Loop landmark of a restaurant, the Berghoff.

Waiters in tuxes, steaming platters of food lifted high, threaded around tables like runners on some absurd obstacle course. The patrons—mostly businessmen, though a few lady shoppers and matinee-goers were mixed in—created a din of conversation and clinking tableware that made every conversation in this wide-open space a private one.

Bill liked to eat, and had accepted my invitation eagerly, even though it had meant driving in from his home on the Northside. Even out of work, he was nattily dressed—dark blue vested suit with wide orange tie with a jeweled stickpin. His jaw jutted, his eyes were dark and sharp, his shoulders broad, his carriage intimidating. Only a pouchiness under his eyes and a touch of gray in his dark thinning hair revealed the stress of recent months.

"I'm goddamn glad you beat the indictment," I said.

He shrugged, buttered up a slice of rye; our Wiener Schnitzel was on the way. "There's still this Grand Jury thing to deal with."

"You'll beat it," I said, but I wasn't so sure. Bill had, in his zeal to nail certain Outfit guys, paid at least one witness to testify. I'd been there when the deal was struck.

"In the meantime," he said cheerfully, "I sit twiddling my thumbs at the old homestead, making the little woman nervous with my unemployed presence."

"You want to do a little work for A-1?"

He shook his head, frowned regretfully. "I'm still a cop, Nate, suspended or not."

"It'd be just between us girls. You still got friends at Town

Hall Station, don't you?"

"Of course."

A waiter old enough to be our father, and looking stern enough to want to spank us, delivered our steaming platters of veal and German fried potatoes and red cabbage.

"I'm working the Keenan case," I said, sipping my beer.

"Still? I figured you'd have dropped out by now." He snorted a laugh. "My brother says you picked up a pretty penny for that interview."

His brother John worked for the *News*.

"Davis met my price," I shrugged. "Look, Bob Keenan seems to want me aboard. Makes him feel better. Anyway, I just intend to work the fringes."

He was giving me his detective look. "That ten grand reward the *Trib* posted wouldn't have anything to do with your decision to stick, would it?"

I smiled and cut my veal. "Maybe. You interested?"

"What can *I* do?"

"First of all, you can clue me in if any of your cop buddies over at Town Hall see any political strings being pulled, or any Outfit strings, either."

He nodded and shrugged, as he chewed; that meant yes.

"Second, you worked the Lipstick killings."

"But I got yanked off, in the middle of the second."

"So play some catch-up ball. Go talk to your buddies. Sort through the files. See if something's slipped through the cracks."

His expression was skeptical. "Every cop in town is on this thing, like ugly on a monkey. What makes you think either one of us can find something *they'd* miss?"

"Bill," I said pleasantly, eating my red cabbage, "we're better detectives than they are."

"True," he said. He cut some more veal. "Anyway, I think

they're going down the wrong road."

"Yeah?"

He shrugged a little. "They're focusing on sex offenders; violent criminals. But look at the M.O. What do you make of it? Who would *you* look for, Nate?"

I'd thought about that a lot. I had an answer ready: "A second-story man. A cat burglar who wasn't stealing for the dough he could find, or the goods he could fence, not primarily. But for the kicks."

Drury looked at me with shrewd, narrowed eyes. "For the kicks. Exactly."

"Maybe a kid. A j.d., or a j.d. who's getting just a little older, into his twenties maybe."

"Why do you say that?"

"Thrill-seeking is a young at heart kind of thing, Bill. And getting in the Johnson woman's apartment took crawling onto a narrow ledge from a fire escape. Took some pretty tricky, almost acrobatic skills. And some recklessness."

He held up his knife. "Plus, it takes strength to jam a bread knife through a woman's neck."

"I'll have to take your word for that. But it does add up to somebody on the young side."

He pointed the knife at me. "I was developing a list of just that kind of suspect . . . only I got pulled off before I could follow up."

I'd hoped for something like this.

"Where's that list now?"

"In my field notes," Drury said. "But let me stop by Town Hall, and nose around a little. Before I give you anything. You want me to check around at Summerdale station, too? I got pals there."

"No," I said. "I already got Kruger, there. He's going to keep me in the know."

"Kruger's okay," Drury said, nodding. "But why's he cooperating with you, Nate?"

The fried potatoes were crisp and salty and fine, but I wished I'd asked for gravy. "That reward the *Trib's* promising. Cops aren't eligible to cash in."

"Ah," Drury said, and drank some dark beer. "Which applies to me, as well."

"Sure. But that's no problem."

"I'm an honest cop, Nate."

"As honest as they come in this town. But you're human. We'll work something out, Bill, you and me."

"We'll start," Bill said, pushing his plate aside, grinning like a goof, "with dessert."

9

That night I stopped in at the funeral home on East Erie. Peg wasn't up to it—felt funny about it, since she'd never met the Keenans; so I went alone. A cop was posted to keep curiosity seekers out, but few made the attempt—the war might have been over, but the memory of personal sorrows was fresh.

The little girl lay dressed in white satin with pink flowers at her breast; you couldn't see the nicks on her face—she was even smiling, faintly. She looked sweetly asleep. She was arranged so that you couldn't tell the arms were still missing.

Norma Keenan had been told, of course, what exactly had happened to her little girl. My compassionate lie had only lessened her sorrow for that first night. Unbelievably, it had gotten worse: the coroner had announced, this afternoon, that there had been "attempted rape."

The parents wore severe black and, while family and friends stood chatting *sotto voce,* were seated to one side. Neither was crying. It wasn't that they were bearing up well: it was shock.

"Thanks for coming, Nate," Bob said, rising, and squeezed my hand. "Will you come to the Mass tomorrow?"

"Sure," I said. It had been a long time since I'd been to Mass; my mother had been Catholic, but she died when I was young.

At St. Gertrude's the next morning, it turned out not to be a Requiem Mass, but the Mass of the Angels, as sung by the one hundred tender voices of the children's choir. "A song of welcome," the priest said, "admitting another to sing before the throne of God."

JoAnn had belonged to this choir; last Christmas, she'd played an angel in the Scared Heart school pageant.

Now she was an armless corpse in a casket at the altar rail; even the beauty of the children's voices and faces, even the long, tapering white candles that cast a flickery golden glow on the little white coffin, couldn't erase that from my mind. When the priest reminded those in attendance that "there is no room for vengeance in our hearts," I bit my tongue. *Speak for yourself, padre.*

People wept openly, men and women alike, many hugging their own children. Some thirteen-hundred had turned out for the Mass, a detail of policemen protected the Keenans as they exited the church. The crowd, however, was well behaved.

And only a handful of us was at the cemetery. The afternoon was overcast, unseasonably chilly, and the wind coursed through All Saint's like a guilty conscience. After a last blessing of holy water from the priest, the little white casket was lowered into a tiny grave protected by a solitary maple. Flowers banking the grave fluttered and danced in the breeze.

I didn't allow myself to cry, not at first. I told myself Keenan was an acquaintance, not a friend; I reminded myself that I had never met the little girl—not before I fished her head out of a goddamn sewer, anyway. I held back the tears, and was a man.

It wasn't till I got home that night, and saw my pregnant wife, that it hit me; knocked the slats right out from under me.

Then I found myself sitting on the couch, crying like a baby, and this time she was comforting me.

It didn't last long, but when it stopped, I came to a strange and disturbing realization: everything I'd been through in this life, from close calls as a cop to fighting Japs in the Pacific, hadn't prepared me for fear like this. For the terror of being a parent. Of knowing something on the planet was so precious to you the very thought of losing it invited madness.

"You're going to help your friend," Peg said. "You're going to get whoever did this."

"I'm going to try, baby," I said, rubbing the wetness away with the knuckles of one hand. "Hell, the combined rewards are up to thirty-six grand."

1 0

The next day, however, I did little on the Keenan case. I did check in with both Kruger and Drury, neither of whom had much for me—nothing that the papers hadn't already told me.

Two janitors had been questioned and considered suspects, briefly. One of them was the old Kraut we'd borrowed the broomstick from—Otto Bergstrum. The other was an Army vet in his early twenties named James Watson, who was the handyman for the nursery from which the kidnap ladder had been stolen. Watson was a prime suspect because, as a juvenile offender, he'd been arrested for molesting an eight-year-old girl.

That long-ago charge had been knocked down to disorderly conduct, however, and meanwhile, back in the present, both Bergstrum and Watson had alibis. Also, they both passed lie-detector tests.

"It doesn't look like there's any significance," Kruger told me on the phone, "to that locker the killer broke into."

"In the so-called 'murder cellar,' you mean?"

"Yeah. Kidnapper stole rags and shopping bags out of it. The guy's clean, whose locker that is."

"Any good prints turn up?"

"No. Not in the murder cellar, or the girl's room. We had two on the window that turned out to be the cleaning lady. We do have a crummy partial off the kidnap note. And we have some picture-frame wire, a loop of it, we found in an alley near the Keenan house; might've been used to strangle the girl. The coroner says she was dead before she was cut up."

"Thank God for that much."

"We have a couple of odd auto sightings, near the Keenan house, in the night and early morning. We're looking into that."

"A car makes sense," I said. "Otherwise, you'd think somebody would've spotted this maniac hand-carrying the body from the Keenans over to that basement."

"I agree. But it was the middle of the night. Time of death, after all, was between one-thirty and two a.m."

Kruger said he'd keep me posted, and that had been that, for me and the Keenan case, on that particular day.

With one rather major exception.

I was about to get into my Plymouth, in a parking garage

near the Rookery, when a dark blue 1946 Mercury slid up and blocked me in.

Before I had the chance to complain, the driver looked out at me and grinned. "Let's take a spin, Heller."

He was a thin-faced, long-chinned, beak-nosed, gray-complected guy about forty; he wasn't big, but his presence was commanding. His name was Sam Flood, and he was a fast-rising Outfit guy, currently Tony Accardo's chauffeur/bodyguard. He was also called "Mooney," which was West Side street slang for nuts.

"A 'spin,' Sam—or a 'ride'?"

Sam laughed. "Come on, Heller. I got a proposition for you. Since when do you turn your nose up at dough?"

I wasn't armed, but it was a cinch Flood was. Flood was a West Side boy, like me, only I grew up around Maxwell Street while he was from the Near West Side's notorious "Patch," and a veteran of the infamous street gang, the 42s.

"Let's talk right here, Sam," I said. "Nobody's around."

He thought about that; his dark eyes glittered. He pretended to like me, but I knew he didn't. He hated all cops, including ex-cops. And my status with the Outfit largely had to do with my one-time friendship with the late Frank Nitti, whom Sam had no particular respect for. Sam was, after all, a protégé of Paul Ricca, who had forced Nitti out.

"Okay," Sam said. He spoke softly, and almost haltingly. "I'm gonna park it right over there in that space. You come sit and talk. Nothing bad's gonna happen to you in my own fuckin' car."

So we sat and talked.

Sam, wearing a dark well-tailored suit and a kelly-green snap-brim, half-turned to look at me. "You know who speaks well of you?"

"Who?"

"Louie Campagna." He thumbed his chest. "I kept an eye on his missus for him while he was in stir on the movie-union rap."

"Louie's all right," I said politely. Campagna had been Nitti's right arm; for some reason, Sam wanted to reassure me that we were pals. Or at least, had mutual pals. Back in '44, I'd encountered Sam for the first time when Outfit treasurer Jake Guzik got kidnapped and I was pulled in as a neutral go-between. From that experience I had learned Sam "Mooney" Flood was one ruthless fucker, and as manipulative as a carnival barker.

"You're on this Keenan case," he said.

That would've tensed me right there, only I was already wound tight.

"Yeah," I said casually. "Not in a big way. The father's a friend, and he wants somebody to keep the cops honest."

That made him laugh. Whether it was the idea of *me* keeping somebody honest, or anybody keeping the cops honest, he didn't say.

I decided to test the waters. "You know why Keenan called me in, don't you?"

"No," Sam said. It seemed a genuine enough response.

"He was afraid the kidnapping might have been the mob getting back at him for not playing ball back east. You know, in his OPA job."

Sam nodded, but then shook his head, no. "That's not likely, Heller. The eastern mobs don't make a play on our turf without checking first."

I nodded; that made sense.

"But just so you know—if you don't already—up to very recent, I was in the gas and food stamp business."

I had known that, which was why seeing the little hood

show up on my figurative doorstep was so chilling; not that meeting with Sam Flood would warm me up under any circumstances.

"But that's over," Sam said. "In fact, it's been over for a couple months. That racket's gone the way of speakeasies. And Heller—when we was in that business, I never, and to my knowledge, no Outfit guy never made no approach to that Keenan guy."

"He never said you did."

The gaunt face relaxed. "Good. Now—let me explain my interest in this case."

"Please do."

"It's looking like that fucking Lipstick Killer did this awful crime on this little child."

"Looks like. But some people think a crank might've written that lipstick message in the alley."

His eyes tightened. "I hear the family received a lipstick letter, too, with the same message: 'Stop me before I kill more' or whatever."

"That's true."

He sighed. Then he looked at me sharply. "Does attorney/ client privilege apply to you and me, if I give you a retainer?"

"Yeah. I'd have to send you a contract with an attorney I work with, to keep it legal. Or we could do it through your attorney. But I don't know that I want you as a client, Sam. No offense."

He raised a finger. "I promise you that working for me will in no way compromise you or put you in conflict of interest with your other client, the Keenan father. If I'm lying, then the deal's off."

I said nothing.

He thrust a fat, sealed envelope into my lap. "That's a grand in fifties."

"Sam, I . . ."

"I'm your client now, Heller. Got that?"

"Well . . ."

"Got it?"

I swallowed and nodded. I slipped the envelope in my inside suitcoat pocket.

"The Lipstick Killer," Sam said, getting us back on the track. "The first victim was a Mrs. Caroline Williams."

I nodded.

He thrust his finger in my face; I looked at it, feeling my eyes cross. It was like looking into a gun barrel. "No one, Heller, no one must know about this." The finger withdrew and the ferret-like gangster sighed and looked out the windshield at the cement wall beyond. "I have a family. Little girls. Got to the protect them. Are you a father, Heller?"

"My wife's expecting."

Sam grinned. "That's great! That's wonderful." Then the grin disappeared. "Look, I'd do anything to protect my Angeline. Some guys, they flaunt their other women. Me, far as my family knows, I never strayed. Never. But . . . you're a man—you understand the needs of a man."

I was starting to get the picture; or at least part of it.

"The thing is, I was seeing this woman, this Caroline Williams. For the most part, it was pretty discreet."

It must have been, if Bill Drury hadn't found out about it; he'd been on that case, after all, and his hate-on for the Outfit was legendary.

As if reading my mind, Sam said, "Not a word to your pal Drury about this! Christ. That guy's nuts."

Mooney should know.

"Anyway, there was this photo of us together. Her and me, together. I want it baçk."

"Not for sentimental reasons, either."

"No," he admitted frankly. "It crushed me that my friend Mrs. Williams had the bad luck to be this maniac's victim. But from what I hear, this guy was not just a sex killer. He was some kind of weirdo second-story man."

"I think so," I said. "I think he was a burglar with a hobby."

"The police reports indicated that stuff was missing. Undergarments, various personal effects. Anyway, even with Drury on the case, I was able to find out that the photo album she had the picture in wasn't among her effects."

"Maybe her family got it."

"I checked that out myself—discreetly."

"Then you think . . . the killer took the photo album?"

Sam nodded. "Yeah. She had photos of herself in bathing suits and shit. If he took her underwear with him, he could've taken that, too."

"So what do you want from me?"

He looked at me hard; he clutched my arm. "All I want is that photo album. Not even that—just that one photo. It was taken in a restaurant, by one of them photo girls who come around."

"How I am supposed to find it?"

"You may find this guy before the cops do. Or, you're tight enough with the cops on the case to maybe get to it before they do. The photo album, I mean. It would embarrass me to have that come out. It would open up an ugly can of worms, and it wouldn't have nothing to do with nothing, where these crackpot killings are concerned. It would hurt me and my family and at the same time only muddy up the waters, where the case against the maniac is concerned."

I thought about that. I had to agree.

"So all you want," I said, "is that photo."

"And your discretion."

"You'd be protected," I said. "It would be through an

attorney, after all. You'd be his client and he would be my client. I couldn't say a word if I wanted to."

"You'll take the job?"

"I already took your money. But what if I don't get results?"

"You keep the retainer. You find and return that picture, you get another four grand."

"What I really want," I said, "is that little girl's murderer. I want to kill that son of a bitch."

"Have all the fun you want," Sam said. "But get me my picture back."

1 1

Lou Sapperstein, who had once been my boss on the pick-pocket detail, was the first man I added when the A-1 expanded. Pushing sixty, Lou had the hard muscular build of a linebacker and the tortoise-shell glasses and bald pate of a scholar; in fact, he was a little of both.

He leaned a palm on my desk in my office. As usual, he was in rolled-up shirtsleeves, his tie loose around his collar. "I spent all morning in the *Trib* morgue—went back a full year."

I had asked Lou to check on any breaking-and-entering cases involving assault on women. It had occurred to me that if, as Drury and I theorized, the Lipstick Killer was a cat burglar whose thrill seeking had escalated to murder, there may have been an intermediate stage, between bloodless break-ins and homicidal ones.

"There are several possibilities," Lou said, "but one jumped right out at me . . ."

He handed me a sheet torn from a spiral pad.

"Katherine Reynolds," I read aloud. Then I read the rest to myself, and said, "Some interesting wrinkles here."

Lou nodded. "Some real similarities. And it happened right smack in between killings number one and two. You think the cops have picked up on it?"

"I doubt it," I said. "This happened on the South Side. The two women who were killed were both on the North Side."

"The little girl, too."

To Chicago cops, such geographic boundaries were inviolate—a North Side case was a North Side case and a crime that happened on the South Side might as well have happened on the moon. Unfortunately, crooks didn't always think that way.

So, late that afternoon, I found myself knocking at the door of the top-floor flat of an eight-story apartment building on the South Side, near the University of Chicago. The building had once been a nurse's dormitory—Billings Hospital was nearby—and most of the residents here still were women in the mercy business.

Like Katherine Reynolds, who was wearing crisp nurse's whites, cap included, when she answered the door.

"Thanks for seeing me on such short notice, Miss Reynolds," I said, as she showed me in.

I'd caught her at the hospital, by phone, and she'd agreed to meet me here at home; she was just getting off.

"Hope I'm not interfering with your supper," I added, hat in hand.

"Not at all, Mr. Heller," she said, unpinning her nurse's cap. "Haven't even started it yet."

She was maybe thirty, a striking brunette, with her hair chopped off in a boyish cut with page-boy bangs; her eyes were large and brown and luminous, her nose pug, her teeth white and slightly, cutely bucked. Her lips were full and scarlet with lipstick. She was slender but nicely curved and just about perfect, except for a slight medicinal smell.

We sat in the living room of the surprisingly large apartment; the furnishings were not new, but they were nice. On the end table next to the couch, where we sat, was a hand-tinted color photographic portrait of a Marine in dress blues, a grinning lantern-jawed young man who looked handsome and dim.

She crossed her legs and the nylons swished. I was a married man, a professional investigator here on business, and her comeliness had no effect on me whatsoever. I put my hat over my hard-on.

"Nice place you got here," I said. "Whole floor, isn't it?"

"Yes," she said. She smiled meaninglessly. "My sister and another girl, both nurses, share it with me. I think this was the head nurse's quarters, back when it was a dorm. All the other flats are rather tiny."

"How long ago was the incident?"

This was one of many questions I'd be asking her that I already knew the answer to.

"You mean the assault?" she said crisply, lighting a cigarette. She exhaled smoke; her lips made a perfect, glistening red O. "About four months ago. The son of a bitch came in through the skylight." She gestured to it. "It must have been around seven a.m. Sis and Dottie were already at work, so I was alone here. I was still asleep . . . actually, just waking up."

"Or did something wake you up?"

"That may have been it. I half-opened my eyes, saw a shadowy figure and then something crashed into my head." She touched her brown boyish hair. "Fractured my skull. I usually wear my hair longer, you know, but they cut a lot of it off."

"Looks good short. Do you know what you were hit with?"

"Your classic blunt instrument. I'd guess a lead pipe. I took a good knock."

"You were unconscious."

"Oh yes. When I woke up, on the floor by the bed, maybe forty minutes later, blood was streaming down my face, and into my eyes. Some of it was sticky, already drying. My apartment was all a kilter. Virtually ransacked. My hands were tied with a lamp cord, rather loosely. I worked myself free, easily. I looked around and some things were missing." She made an embarrassed face, gestured with a cigarette in hand. "Underwear. Panties. Bras. But also a hundred and fifty bucks were gone from my purse."

"Did you call the police at that point?"

"No. That's when I heard the knock at the door. I staggered over there and it was a kid—well, he could've been twenty, but I'd guess eighteen. He had dark hair, long and greased back. Kind of a good-looking kid. Like a young Cornell Wilde. Looked a little bit like a juvenile delinquent, or anyway, like a kid trying to look like one and not quite pulling it off."

"What do you mean?"

"Well, he wore a black leather jacket, and a T-shirt and dungarees . . . but they looked kind of new. Too clean. More like a costume than clothing."

"What did he want?"

"He said he was a delivery boy—groceries, and he was looking for the right apartment to make his delivery."

"He was lost."

"Yes, but we didn't spend much time discussing that. He took one look at my bloody face and said he would get some help right away."

"And did he?"

She nodded; exhaled smoke again. "He found the building

manager, told him the lady in the penthouse flat was injured, and needed medical attention. And left."

"And the cops thought he might have been the one who did it? Brought back by a guilty conscience?"

"Yes. But I'm not sure I buy that."

I nodded. But to me it tied in: the murderer who washed and bandaged his victims' wounds displayed a similar misguided *stop-me-catch-me* remorse. Even little JoAnn's body parts had been cleansed—before they were disposed of in sewers.

"The whole thing made me feel like a jerk," she said.

That surprised me. "Why?"

She lifted her shoulders; it did nice things to her cupcake breasts. Yes, I know. I'm a heel. "Well, if only I'd reacted quicker, I might have been able to protect myself. I mean, I've had all sorts of self-defense training."

"Oh?"

She flicked ashes into a glass tray on the couch arm. "I'm an army nurse—on terminal leave. I served overseas. European theater."

"Ah."

She gave me a sly smile. "You were in the Pacific, weren't you?"

"Well, uh, yes."

"I read about you in the papers. I recognized your name right away. You're kind of well known around town."

"Don't believe everything you read in the papers, Miss Reynolds."

"You won the Silver Star, didn't you?"

I was getting embarrassed. I nodded.

"So did Jack."

"Jack?"

"My husband. He was a marine, too. You were on Guadalcanal?"

"Yes."

"So was Jack." She smiled. Then the smile faded and she sucked smoke in again. "Only he didn't come back."

"Lot of good men didn't. I'm sorry."

She made a dismissive gesture with a red-nailed hand. "Mr. Heller, why are you looking into this?"

"I think it may relate to another case; that's all."

"The Lipstick Killer?"

I hesitated, then nodded. "But I'd appreciate it if you didn't say anything about it to anybody just yet."

"Why haven't the cops done anything about this?"

"You mean, the Lipstick Killer, or what happened to you?"

"Both! And, why have *you* made this connection, when they haven't?"

I shrugged. "Maybe I'm more thorough. Or maybe I'm just grasping at straws."

"Well, it occurred to *me* there might be a connection. You'd think it would've occurred to the police, too!"

"You'd think."

"You know, there's something . . . never mind."

"What?"

She shook her head, tensed her lips. "There was something . . . creepy . . . that I never told anybody about." She looked at me with eyes impossibly large, so dark brown the pupils were lost. "But I feel like I can talk to you."

She touched my hand. Hers was warm. Mine felt cold.

"On the floor . . . in the bathroom . . . I found something. Something I just . . . cleaned up. Didn't tell anybody about. It embarrassed me."

"You're a nurse . . ."

"I know. But I was embarrassed just the same. It was . . . come."

"What?"

"There was come on the floor. You know—ejaculate. Semen."

12

When I got home, I called Drury and told him about Katherine Reynolds.

"I think you may be on to something," Drury said. "You should tell Lt. Kruger about this."

"I'll call him tomorrow. But I wanted to give you the delivery boy's description first—see if it rang any bells."

Drury made a clicking sound. "Lot of kids in those black leather jackets these days. Don't know what the world's coming to. Lot of kids trying to act like they're in street gangs, even when they're not."

"Could he be a University of Chicago student?"

"Pulling crimes on the North Side?"

Even a cop as good as Drury wore the geographical blinders.

"Yeah," I said. "There's this incredible new mode of transportation they call the El. It's just possible our boy knows about it."

Drury ignored the sarcasm. "Lot of greasy-haired would-be under-age hoods around, Nate. Doesn't really narrow the field much."

"That look like a young Cornell Wilde?"

"That want to," Drury said, "yes."

We sighed, and hung up.

Eavesdropping, Peg was half in the kitchen, half in the hall. She wore a white apron over the swell of her tummy. She'd made meat loaf. The smell of it beckoned. Despite herself, Peg was a hell of a cook.

"Good looking?" she asked.

"What?"

"This nurse you went and talked to," she said.

"Oh. I didn't notice."

She smirked; went back into the kitchen. I followed. I waited at the table while she stirred gravy.

"Blonde?" she asked, her back to me.

"No. Brunette, I think."

She looked over her shoulder at me. "You think?"

"Brunette."

"Nice and slender, I'll bet. With a nice shape. Not fat and sloppy. Not a cow. Not an elephant."

"Peg . . ."

She turned; her wooden spoon dripped brown gravy onto the linoleum. "I'm going crazy out here, Nate. I'm ugly, and I'm bored."

"You're not ugly. You're beautiful."

"Fuck you, Heller! I'm an ugly cow, and I'm *bored* out here in the sticks. Jesus, couldn't we live someplace where there's somebody for me to talk to?"

"We have neighbors."

"Squirrels, woodchucks and that dip down the street who mows his lawn on the even days and washes his car on the odd. It's all vacant lots and nurseries and prairie out here. Why couldn't we live closer to the city? I feel like I'm living in a goddamn pasture. Which is where a cow like me belongs, I suppose."

I stood. I went to her and held her. She was angry, but she let me.

She didn't look at me as she bit off the words. "You go off to the Loop and you can be a businessman and you can be a detective and you have your co-workers and your friends and contacts and interview beautiful nurses and you make the papers and you're living a real life. Not stuck out here in a box with a lawn. Listening to 'Ma Perkins.' Peeling potatoes. Ironing shirts."

"Baby . . ."

She thumped her chest with a forefinger. "I used to have a life. I was a professional woman. I was an executive secretary."

"I know, I know."

"Nate—Nate, I'm afraid."

"Afraid?"

"Afraid I'm not cut out to be a housewife. Afraid I'm not cut out to be a mother."

I smiled at her gently; touched her face the same way. Touched her tummy. "You're already a mother, by definition. Give it a chance. The kid will change things. The neighborhood will grow."

"I hate it here."

"Give it a year. You don't like it, we'll move. Closer to town."

She smiled tightly, bravely. Nodded. Turned back to the stove.

The meal was good. We had apple pie, which may have been sarcasm on Peg's part, but if so it was delicious sarcasm. We chatted about business; about family. After the tension, things got relaxed.

We were cuddled on the couch listening to big band music on the radio when the phone rang. It was Drury again.

"Listen," he said, "sorry to bother you, but I've been thinking, and something did jog loose, finally."

"Swell! What?"

"There was this kid I busted a few years back. He was nice-looking, dark-haired, but kind of on the hoody side, though he had a good family. His dad was a security guard with a steel mill. Anyway, the boy was a good student, a bright kid—only for kicks, he stole. Furs, clothes, jewelry, old coins, guns."

"You were working out of Town Hall Station at the time?"

"Yeah. All his robberies were on the North Side. He was just thirteen."

"How old is he now?"

"Seventeen."

"Then this was a while ago."

"Yeah, but I busted him again, on some ten burglaries, two years ago. He's agile, Nate—something of human fly, navigating ledges, fire escapes . . . going in windows."

"I see."

"Anyway, he did some time at Gibault." That was a correctional institution for boys at Terre Haute. "But supposedly he came out reformed. He's a really good student—so good, at seventeen, he's a sophomore in college."

"At the University of Chicago?" I said.

"Yeah," Drury said. "And guess what his part-time job is?"

"Delivery boy," I said.

"What a detective you are," Drury said.

13

Jerome Lapps, precocious seventeen-year-old sophomore science student, resided at a dormitory on the University of Chicago campus.

On the phone Drury had asked, "You know where his folks live?"

"What, you take me for a psychic?"

"You could've tripped over this kid, Nate. The Lapps family lives in Lincolnwood."

He gave me the address; not so far from Peg and me.

Sobering as that was, what was more interesting was that the kid lived at school, not home; even during summer session. Specifically, he was in Gates Hall on the Midway campus.

The Midway, a mile-long block-wide parkway between 59th and 60th, connected Washington and Jackson parks, and served to separate Hyde Park and the university eggheads from the real South Side. Just beyond the Midway were the Gothic limestone buildings and lushly landscaped acres of the university. At night the campus looked like another world. Of course, it looked like another world in the daylight, too.

But this was night, and the campus seemed largely deserted. That was partly summer, partly not. I left the Plymouth in a quadrangle parking lot and found my way to the third floor of Gates Hall, where I went to Lapps' room and knocked on the door. No answer. I knocked again. No answer. The door was locked.

A student well into his twenties—probably a vet on the G.I. Bill—told me where to find the grad student who was the resident assistant in charge of that floor.

The resident assistant leaned against the door jamb of his room with a bottle of beer in his hand and his shirt half-tucked in. His hair was red, his eyes hooded, his mouth smirky. He was perhaps twenty years old.

"What can I do for you, bud?" the kid asked.

"I'm Jerry Lapps' uncle. Supposed to meet him at his room, but he's not in."

"Yeah?"

"You got a key? I'd like to wait inside."

He shrugged. "Against the rules."

"I'm his uncle Abraham," I said. And I showed him a five-dollar bill. "I'm sure it'll be okay."

The redheaded kid brightened; his eyes looked almost awake. He snatched the five-spot and said, "Ah. Honest Abe. Jerry mentioned you."

He let me into Lapps' room and went away.

Judging by the pair of beds, one against either wall, Jerome Lapps had a roommate. But the large single room accommodated two occupants nicely. One side was rather spartan and neat as a boot-camp barracks, while across the room an unmade bed was next to a plaster wall decorated with pictures of baseball players and heart-throb movie actors. Each side of the room had its own writing desk, and again, one was cluttered, while the other was neat.

It didn't take long to confirm my suspicion that the messy side of the room belonged to the seventeen-year-old. Inside the calculus text on the sloppy desk, the name Jerome C. Lapps was written on the flyleaf in a cramped hand. The handwriting on a notepad, filled with doodles, looked the same; written several times, occasionally underlined, were the words: "Rogers Park."

Under Jerome C. Lapps' bed were three suitcases.

In one suitcase were half of the panties and bras in the city of Chicago.

The other suitcase brimmed with jewelry, watches, two revolvers, one automatic, and a smaller zippered pouch of some kind, like an oversize shaving kit. I unzipped it and recoiled.

It was a medical kit, including hypos, knives and a surgical saw.

I put everything back and stood there and swallowed and tried to get the image of JoAnn Keenan's doll-like head out of my mind. The best way to do that was to get back to work, which I did, proceeding to the small closet on Jerome's side of the room. On the upper shelf I found a briefcase.

I opened it on the neater bed across the way. Inside were several thousand bucks in war bonds and postal savings certificates. He'd apparently put any cash he'd stolen into these, and any money from fenced goods, although considering that well-stuffed suitcase of jewelry and such, I couldn't imagine he'd bothered to fence much if any of what he'd taken.

As typically teen-ager sloppy as his side of the dorm room was, Jerry had neatly compartmentalized his booty: ladies underwear in one bag; jewelry and watches in another; paper goods in the briefcase. Included in the latter were clipped photos of big-shot Nazis. Hitler, Goering and Goebbels.

Jerry had some funny fucking heroes.

Finally, in the briefcase, was a photo album. Thumbing through it, I saw photos of an attractive woman, frequently in a bathing suit and other brief, summer apparel. There was also a large photo of the same woman with a ferret-faced male friend in a nightclub setting; you could see a table of men sitting behind them as well, clearly, up a tier. A sweet and tender memento of Caroline Williams and Sam Flood's love affair.

I removed the photo, folded it without creasing it, and slipped it into my inside suitcoat pocket. I put the photo album back, closed up the briefcase and was returning it to the upper shelf of the closet when the dorm-room door opened.

"What the hell are you doing?" a male voice demanded.

I was turning around and slipping my hand under my jacket to get at my gun, at the same time, but the guy reacted fast. His hand must have hit the light switch, because the room went black and I could hear him coming at me, and then he was charging into me.

I was knocked back into the corner, by the many-paned windows, through which some light was filtering, and I saw a thin face, its teeth clenched, as the figure pressed into me and a single fist was smashing into my stomach, powerfully.

The damn guy was almost sitting on me, and I used all my strength to lift up and lift him off, heaving him bodily onto the floor. He was scrambling to his feet when I stuck the nine millimeter in his face and said, "Don't."

Somebody hit the lights.

It was the red-headed dorm assistant. Even drunk, he didn't like the looks of this.

Neither did I: the guy in front of me was not Jerome Lapps, but a slender, tow-headed fellow in his mid-twenties. The empty sleeve of his left arm was tucked into a sportcoat pocket.

I was a hell of a tough character: I'd just bested a cripple. Of course, I had to pull a gun to do it.

"What the hell . . ." the red-headed kid began. His eyes were wide at the sight of the gun in my hand. The one-armed guy in front of me seemed less impressed.

"Police officer," I said to the redhead. "Go away."

He swallowed, nodded, and went.

"You're Jerome's roommate?" I asked the one-armed fellow.

"Yeah. Name's Robinson. Who are you? You really a cop?"

"I run a private agency," I said. "What branch were you in?"

"Army."

I nodded. "Marines," I said. I put the gun away "You got a smoke?"

He nodded; with the one hand he had left, he got some Chesterfields out of his sportcoat pocket. Shook one out for me, then another for himself. He put the Chesterfields back and got out a silver Zippo. He lit us both up. He was goddamn good with that hand.

"Thank God them bastards left me with my right," he grinned sheepishly.

He sat on his bed. I sat across from him on Lapps'.

We smoked for a while. I thought about a punk kid cutting out pin-ups of Hitler while sharing a room with a guy who lost an arm over there. I was so happy I'd fought for the little fucker's freedoms.

"You're looking for Jerry, aren't you?" he asked. His eyes were light blue and sadder than a Joan Crawford picture.

"Yeah."

He shook his head. "Figured that kid would get himself into trouble."

"You roomed with him long?"

"Just for summer session. He's not a bad kid. Easy to get along with. Quiet."

"You know what he's got under his bed?"

"No."

"Suitcases full of stolen shit. If you need a new wristwatch, you picked the right roomie."

"I didn't know he was doing anything like that."

"Then what made you think he was going to get himself in trouble?"

"That black leather jacket of his."

"Huh?"

He shrugged. "When he'd get dressed up like a juvie. That black leather jacket. Dungarees. White T-shirt. Smoking cigarettes." He sucked on his own cigarette, shook his head. "He'd put that black leather jacket on, not every night, more like every once in a while. I'd ask him where he was going. You know what he'd say?"

"No."

"On the prowl."

I thought about that.

"Is his black leather jacket hanging in that closet you were lookin' in?"

"No," I said.

"Then guess where he is right now."

"On the prowl," I said.

He nodded.

14

Now I was on the prowl.

I went up Lakeshore, turned onto Sheridan and followed it up to the Loyola El stop. The notepad on Lapps' desk had sent me here, to Rogers Park, the northernmost neighborhood in Chicago; beyond was Evanston. Here, in a three-block wide and fourteen-block long band between the lake and the El tracks was the middle-class residential area that would suit the kid's M.O.

Lapps seemed partial to a certain type of building; according to Drury, many of the boy's burglaries were pulled off in tall, narrow apartment buildings consisting of small studio apartments. Same was true of where the two women who'd been killed had lived, and Katherine Reynolds, too.

First I would look for the dark-haired, black-leather-jacketed Lapps around the El stops—he had no car—and then I would cruise the side streets off Sheridan, looking in particular for that one type of building.

Windows rolled down, half-leaned out, I crawled slowly along, cutting the Plymouth's headlights as I cruised the residential neighborhoods; that way I didn't announce myself, and I seemed to be able to eyeball the sidewalks and buildings better that way. Now and then another car blinked its brights at me, but I ignored them and cruised on through the unseasonably cool July night.

About two blocks down from the Morse Avenue business district, on a street of modest apartment buildings, I spotted two guys running back the direction I'd come. The one in the lead was a heavy-set guy in his T-shirt; close on his heels was a fellow in a plaid shirt. At first I thought one was chasing the other, but then it was clear they were together, and very upset.

The heavy-set guy was slowing down and gesturing with open hands. "Where d'he go? Where d'he go?"

The other guy caught up to him and they both slowed down; in the meantime, I pulled over and trotted over to them.

"The cops, already!" the heavy-set guy said joyously. He was a bald guy in his forties; five o'clock shadow smudged his face.

I didn't correct their assumption that I was a cop. I merely asked, "What gives, gents?"

The guy in the plaid shirt, thin, in his thirties, glasses, curly hair, pointed at nothing in particular and said, in a rush, "We had a prowler in the building. He was in my neighbor's flat!"

"I'm the janitor," the fat guy said, breathing hard, hands on his sides, winded. "I caught up to the guy in the lobby, but he pulled a gun on me." He shook his head. "Hell, I got a wife in the hospital, and three kids, that all need me unventilated. I let 'im pass."

"But Bud went and got reinforcements," the thin guy said, taking over, pointing to himself, "and my wife called the cops. And we took chase."

That last phrase almost made me smile, but I said, "Was it a dark-haired kid in a black leather jacket?"

They both blinked and nodded, properly amazed.

"He's going to hop the El," I said. I pointed to the thin guy. "You take the Morse El stop, I'll . . ."

A scream interrupted me.

We turned toward the scream and it became a voice, a woman's voice, yelling, "He's up *there!*"

We saw her then, glimpsed between two rather squat apartment houses: a stout, older woman, lifting her skirts almost daintily as she barrelled down the alley. I ran back there; the two guys were trailing well behind, and not eagerly. A lame horse could have gained the same lead.

The fleeing woman saw me, and we passed each other. She looked back and pointed, without missing a step, saying, "Up on the second-floor porch!" Then she continued on with her escape.

It would have been a comic moment, if the alley hadn't been so dark and I hadn't been both running and scrambling for my nine millimeter.

I slowed to face the back yard of a two-story brick building and its exposed wooden rear stairways and porches. Despite what the fleeing woman had said, the second-floor porch seemed empty, though it was hard to tell: it was dark back here, the El tracks looming behind me, casting their shadow. Maybe she meant the next building down. . . .

As I was contemplating that, a figure rose on the second-floor porch and pointed a small revolver at me and I could see the hand moving, he was pulling the trigger, but his gun wasn't firing, wasn't working.

Mine was. I squeezed off three quick rounds and the latticework wood near him got chewed up, splinters flying. I didn't know if I'd hit him or not, and didn't wait to see; I moved for those steps, and bolted up one flight, and was at the bottom of the second when the figure loomed up above me, at the top of

71 ◆

the stairs, and I saw him, his pale handsome face under long black greasy hair, his black leather jacket, his dungarees, and he threw the revolver at me like a baseball, and I ducked to one side, and swung my nine millimeter up just as he leaped.

He knocked me back before I could fire, back through the railing of the first-floor porch, snapping it into pieces like so many matchsticks, and we landed in a tangle on the grass, my gun getting lost on the trip. Then he was on top of me, like he was fucking me, and he was a big kid, powerful, pushing me down, pinning me like a wrestler, his teeth clenched, his eyes wide and maniacal.

I heaved with all my strength and weight and pitched him off to one side, but he didn't lose his grip on me, and we rolled, and I was on top now, only he hadn't given up, he hadn't let go, he had me more than I had him and that crazed, glazed look on his face scared the shit out of me. I couldn't punch him, even though I seemed to have the advantage, couldn't get my arms free, and he rocked up, as if he wanted to take a bite out of my face.

I was holding him down, but it was a standoff at best.

Then I sensed somebody coming up—that janitor and his skinny pal, maybe.

But the voice I heard didn't belong to either of them: "Is that the prowler?"

Still gripping my powerful captive by his arms, I glanced up and saw hovering over us a burly guy in swimming trunks holding a clay flower pot in his hands.

"That's him," I said, struggling.

"That's all I wanted to know," the burly guy said, and smashed the flower pot over the kid's head.

15

On the third smack, the flower pot—which was empty—shattered into fragments and the kid's eyes rolled back and went round and white and blank like Orphan Annie's, and then he shut them. Blood was streaming down the kid's pale face. He was ruggedly handsome, even if Cornell Wilde was stretching it.

I got off him and gulped for my breath and the guy in his bathing trunks said, "Neighbors said a cop was after a prowler."

I stuck my hand out. "Thanks, buddy. I didn't figure the cavalry would show up in swim trunks, but I'll take what I can get."

His grasp was firm. He was an affable-looking, open-faced, hairy-chested fellow of maybe thirty-five. We stood over the unconscious kid like hunters who just bagged a moose.

"You a cop?"

"Private," I said. "My name's Nate Heller."

He grinned. "I thought you looked familiar. You're Bill Drury's pal, aren't you? I'm Chet Dickinson—I work traffic in the Loop."

"You're a cop? What's that, summer uniform?"

He snorted a laugh. "I live around here. My family and me was just walking back from a long day at the beach, when we run into this commotion. I sent Grace and the kids on home and figured I better check it out. Think we ought to get this little bastard to a hospital?"

I nodded. "Edgewater's close. Should we call for an ambulance? I got a car."

"You mind? The son of a bitch could have a concussion." He laughed again. "I saw you two strugglin', and I grabbed that flower pot off a window sill. Did the trick."

"Sure did."

"Fact, I mighta overdid it."

"Not from my point of view."

After Dickinson had found and collected the kid's revolver and contributed his beach towel to wrap the kid's head in, we drunk-walked Lapps to my car.

The burly bare-chested cop helped me settle the boy in the rider's seat. "I'll run over home, and call in, and get my buggy, and meet you over at Edgewater."

"Thanks. You know, I used to work traffic in the Loop."

"No kiddin'. Small world."

I had cuffs in the glove box; I cuffed the unconscious kid's hands behind him, in case he was faking it. I looked at the pleasant-faced cop. "Look—if anything comes of this, you got a piece of the reward action. It'll be just between us."

"Reward action?"

I put a hand on his hairy shoulder. "Chet—we just caught the goddamn Lipstick Killer."

His jaw dropped and I got in and pulled away, while he ran off, looking in those trunks of his like somebody in a half-assed track meet.

Then I pulled over around a corner and searched the kid. I figured there was no rush getting him to the hospital. If he died, he died.

He had two five-hundred-buck postal savings certificates in a pocket of his leather jacket. In his billfold, which had a University of Chicago student I.D. card in the name Jerome C. Lapps, was a folded-up letter, typed. It was dated last month. It said:

Jerry—

I haven't heard from you in a long time. Tough luck about the jail term. You'll know better next time.

I think they're catching up to me, so I got to entrust
some of my belongings to you. I'll pick these suitcases
up later. If you get short of cash, you can dip into the
postal certificates.
 I appreciate you taking these things off my hands
when I was being followed. Could have dumped it, but
I couldn't see losing all that jewelry. I'll give you a
phone call before I come for the stuff.

George

I was no handwriting expert, but the handwritten signature
sure looked like Lapps' own cramped handwriting from the
inside cover of his calculus book.

The letter struck me immediately as a lame attempt on the
kid's part to blame the stolen goods stashed in his dorm room
on some imaginary accomplice. Carrying it around with him,
yet—an alibi in his billfold.

He was stirring.

He looked at me. Blinked. His lashes were long. "Who are
you, mister? Where am I?"

I threw a sideways forearm into his stomach and doubled
him over. He let the air out with a groan of pain that filled the
car and made me smile.

"I'm somebody you tried to shoot, is who I am," I said.
"And where you are is up shit creek without a paddle."

He shook his head, licked his lips. "I don't remember trying
to shoot anybody. I'd never do a thing like that."

"Oh? You pointed a revolver at me, and when it wouldn't
shoot, you hurled it at me. Then you jumped me. This just
happened, Jerry."

A comma of greasy black hair fell to his forehead.

"You . . . you know my name? Oh. Sure." He noticed his
open billfold on the seat next to us.

"I knew you before I saw your I.D., Jerry. I been on your trail all day."

"I thought you cops worked in pairs."

"I don't work for the city. Right now, I'm working for the Robert Keenan family."

He recognized the name—anybody in Chicago would have—but his reaction was one of confusion, not alarm, or guilt, or anything else I might have expected.

"What does that have to do with me, mister?"

"You kidnapped their little girl, Jerry—you strangled her and then you tried to fuck her and then you cut her in pieces and threw the pieces in the sewer."

"What . . . what are you . . ."

I sidearmed him in the stomach again. I wanted to shove his head against the dash, but after those blows to the skull with that flower pot, it might kill him. I wasn't particularly interested in having him die in my car. Get blood all over my new Plymouth. Peg would have a fit.

"You're the Lipstick Killer, Jerry. And I caught you going up the back stairs, like the cheap little sneak thief you are."

He looked down at his lap, guiltily. "I didn't kill those women."

"Really. Who did?"

"George."

The letter. The alibi.

"George," I said.

"Yeah," he said. "George did it."

"George did it."

"Sometimes I went along. Sometimes I helped him prepare. But I never did it. George did."

"Is that how you're going to play it?"

"George did it, mister. George hurt those women."

"Did George jack off on the floor, or did you, Jerry?"

Now he started to cry.

"I did that," he admitted. "But George did the killings."

"JoAnn Keenan too?"

Lapps shook his head; his face glistened with tears. "He must have. He must have."

16

Cops in uniform, and plainclothes too, were waiting at the hospital when I deposited Lapps at the emergency room. I didn't talk to the kid after that, though I stuck around, at the request of a detective from Rogers Park.

The word spread fast. Dickinson, when he called it in, had spilled the Lipstick Killer connection. The brass started streaming in, and Chief of Detectives Storm took me off to one side and complimented me on my fine work. We decided that my visit to Lapps' dorm room would be off the record for now; in the meantime, South Side detectives were already on the scene making the same discoveries I had, only with the proper warrants.

I got a kick out of being treated like somebody special by the Chicago police department. Storm and even Tubbo Gilbert were all smiles and arms around my shoulder, when the press showed, which they quickly did. For years I'd been an "ex-cop" who left the force under a cloud in the Cermak adminis-tration; now I was a "distinguished former member of the Detective Bureau who at one time was the youngest plain-clothes officer on the force."

It soon became a problem, having the emergency area clogged with police personnel, politicians and reporters. Lapps was moved upstairs, and everybody else moved to the lobby.

Dickinson, when he'd gone home, had taken time to get out of his trunks and into uniform, which was smart; the flash-bulbs were popping around the husky, amiable patrolman. We posed for a few together, and he whispered to me, "We done good."

"You and your flower pot."

"You're a hell of cop, Heller. I don't care what anybody says."

That was heartwarming.

My persistent pal Davis of the *News* was among the first of the many reporters to arrive and he buttonholed me with an offer of a grand for an exclusive. Much as I hated to, I had to turn him down.

From his expression you'd think I'd pole-axed him. "Heller turning down a pay-off? Why?"

"This is too big to give to one paper. I got to let the whole world love me this time around." Most of the reward money—which was up to forty grand, now—had been posted by the various newspapers (though the city council had anted up, too) and I didn't want to alienate anybody.

"It's gonna be months before you see any of that dough," Davis whined. "It's all contingent upon a conviction, you know."

"I know. I can wait. I'm a patient man. Besides, I got a feeling the A-1 isn't going to be hurting for business after this."

Davis smirked. "Feelin' pretty cocky aren't you? Pretty smug."

"That's right," I said, and brushed by him. I went to the pay phones and called home. It was almost ten, but Peg usually stayed up at least that late.

"Nate! Where have you been . . . it's almost . . ."

"I know. I got him."

"What?"

"I got him."

There was a long pause.

"I love you," she said.

That beat reward money all to hell.

"I love you, too," I said. "Both of you."

I was slipping out of the booth when Lieutenant Kruger shambled over. His mournful-hound puss was twisted up in a grin. He extended his hand and we shook vigorously.

He took my arm, spoke in my ear. "Did you take a look at the letter in Lapps' billfold?"

I nodded. "It's his spare-tire of an alibi. He told me 'George' did the killings. Is he sticking to that story?"

Kruger nodded. "Only I don't think there is a George."

"Next you'll be spoiling Santa Claus and the Easter Bunny for me."

"I don't think that's what he's up to."

"Oh? What is he up to, lieutenant?"

"I think it's a Jekyll and Hyde routine."

"Oh. *He's* George, only he doesn't know it. Split personality. There's a post-war scam for you."

Kruger nodded. "Insanity plea."

"The papers will love that shit."

"They love the damnedest things." He grinned again. "Tonight they even love you."

Chief of Detectives Storm came and found me, shortly after that, and said, "There's somebody who wants to talk to you."

He led me back behind the reception counter to a phone, and

he smiled quietly as he handed me the receiver. He might have been presenting an award of valor.

"Nate?" the voice said.

"Bob?"

"Nate. God bless you, Nate. You found the monster. You found him."

"It's early yet. The real investigation has just started . . ."

"I knew I did the right thing calling you. I knew it."

I could tell he was crying.

"Bob. You give Norma my love."

"Thank you, Nate. Thank you."

I didn't know what to say. So I just said, "Thanks, Bob. Good night."

I gave a few more press interviews, made an appointment with Storm to come to First District Station the next morning and give a formal statement, shook Kruger's hand again, and wandered out into the parking lot. Things were winding down. I slipped behind the wheel of my Plymouth and was about to start the engine when I saw the face in my rear-view mirror.

"Hello, Heller," the man said.

His face was all sharp angles and holes: cheek-bones, pock-marks, sunken dead eyes, pointed jaw, dimpled chin. His suit was black and well tailored—like an undertaker with style. His arms were folded, casually, and he was wearing kid gloves. In the summer.

He was one of Sam Flood's old cronies, a renowned thief from the 42 gang in the Patch. Good with a knife. His last name was Morello.

"We need to talk," he said. "Drive a while."

His first name was George.

17

"Sam couldn't come himself," George said. "Sends his regards, and apologies."

We were on Sheridan, heading toward Evanston.

"I was going to call Sam when I got home," I said, watching him in the rearview mirror. His eyes were gray under bushy black brows; spooky fucking eyes.

"Then you did make it to the kid's pad, before the cops." George sighed; smiled. A smile on that slash of a craggy face was not a festive thing.

"Yeah."

"And you got what Sam wants?"

"I do."

"The photo?"

"Yes."

"That's swell. You're all right, Heller. You're all right. Pull over into the graveyard, will you?"

Calvary Cemetery was the sort of Gothic graveyard where Bela Lugosi and Frankenstein's monster might go for a stroll. I pulled in under the huge limestone archway and, when George directed, pulled off the main path onto a side one, and slowed to a stop. I shut the engine off. The massive granite wall of the cemetery muffled the roar of traffic on Sheridan; the world of the living seemed suddenly very distant.

"What's this about, George?" At Statesville, they say, where he was doing a stretch for grand-theft auto, George was the prison shiv artist; an iceman whose price was five cartons of smokes, for which an individual that was annoying you became deceased.

Tonight George's voice was pleasant; soothing. A Sicilian disc jockey. "Sam just wants his photo, that's all."

"What's the rush?"

"Heller—what's it to you?"

"I'd rather turn it over to Sam personally."

He unfolded his arms and revealed a silenced Luger in his gloved right hand. "Sam says you should give it to me."

"It's in the trunk of the car."

"The trunk?"

"I had the photo in my coat pocket, but when I realized cops were going to be crawling all over, I slipped it in an envelope in my trunk, with some other papers."

That was the truth. I did that at the hospital, before I took Lapp inside.

"Show me," George said.

We got out of the car. George made me put my hands up and, gun in his right hand, he calmly patted me down with his left. He found the nine millimeter under my arm, slipped it out and tossed it gently through the open window of the Plymouth onto the driver's seat.

Calvary was a rich person's cemetery, with mausoleums and life-size statues of dear departed children and other weirdness, all casting their shadows in the moonlight. George kept the gun in hand, but he wasn't obnoxious about it. I stepped around back of the Plymouth, unlocked the trunk and reached in. George took a step forward. I doubled him over with the tire iron, then whacked the gun out of his hand, and swung the iron sideways against his cheek as he began to rise up.

I picked up his Luger and put a knee on his chest and the nose of the silenced gun against his bloody cheekbone. I would have to kill him. There was little doubt of that. His gray eyes were narrowed and full of hate and chillingly absent of fear.

"Was killing me Sam's idea, or yours?"

"Who said anything about killing you?"

I forced the bulky silenced nose of the gun into his mouth. Time for the Chicago lie-detector test.

Fear came into his eyes, finally.

I removed the gun, slowly, not taking any teeth, and said, "Your idea or Sam's?"

"Mine."

"Why, George?"

"Fuck you, Heller."

I put the gun in his mouth again.

After I removed it, less gently this time, cutting the roof of his mouth, he said through bloody spittle, "You're a loose end. Nobody likes loose ends."

"What's it to you, George?"

He said nothing; he was shaking. Most of it was anger. Some of it was fear. An animal smell was coming up off him.

"I said, what's it to you, George? What was your role in it?"

His eyes got very wide; something akin to panic was in them.

And then I knew.

Don't ask me how, exactly, but I did.

"You killed her," I said. It was part question, part statement. "*You* killed Sam's girl friend. For Sam?"

He thought about the question; I started to push the gun back in his mouth and he began to nod, lips kissing the barrel. "It was an accident. Sam threw her over, and she was posing a problem."

I didn't ask whether that problem was blackmail or going to the press or cops or what. It didn't much matter.

"So he had you hit her?"

"It was a fuck-up. I was just supposed to put the fear of God in her and get that fucking picture."

I pressed the gun into his cheek; the one that wasn't bloody. "That kid—Lapps . . . he was your accomplice?"

83 ◆

"No! I didn't know who the hell he was. If we knew who he was, we coulda got that photo long time ago. Why the fuck you think *you* were hired?"

That made sense; but not much else did. "So what was the deal, George?"

His eyes tightened; his expression said: *You know how it is.* "I was slapping her around, trying to get her to tell me where that picture was. I'd already tossed the place, but just sorta half-ass. She was arrogant. Spitting at me. All of a sudden her throat got cut."

Accidents will happen. "How did that kid get the photo album, then?"

"I heard something at the window; I looked up and saw this dark shape there, out on the fire escape . . . thought it was a cop or something."

The black leather jacket.

"I thought *fuck it* and cut out," he said. "The kid must've come in, stole some shit, found that photo album someplace I missed, and left with it and a bunch of other stuff."

But before that, he washed the victim's wounds and applied a few bandages.

"What about the second girl?" I demanded. "Margaret Johnson? And the Keenan child?"

"I had nothing to do with them crimes. You think I'm a fuckin' psycho?"

I thought that one best left unanswered.

"George," I said calmly, easing the gun away from his face, "you got any suggestions on how we can resolve our differences, here? Can you think of some way both of us can walk out of this graveyard tonight?"

He licked his lips. Smiled a ghastly, blood-flecked smile. "Let bygones be bygones. You don't tell anybody what you know—Sam included—and I just forget about you working me over. That's fair. That's workable."

I didn't see where he got the knife; I hadn't seen a hand slip into a pocket at all. He slashed through my sleeve, but didn't cut me. When I shot him in the head, his skull exploded, but almost none of him got on me. Just my gun hand. A limestone angel, however, got wreathed in blood and brains.

I lifted up off him and stood there panting for a while. The sounds of muted traffic reminded me there was a world to go back to. I checked his pockets, found some Camels and lit one up; kept the pack. Then I wiped my prints off his gun, laid it near him, retrieved my tire iron, put it back in the trunk, which I closed up, and left him there with his peers.

18

The phone call came late morning, which was a good thing: I didn't even make it into the office till after ten.

"You were a busy fella yesterday, Heller," Sam Flood's voice said cordially.

"I get around, Sam."

"Papers are full of you. Real hero. There's other news, though, that hasn't made the papers yet."

"By the afternoon edition, it'll be there."

We each knew what the other was talking about: soon Giorgio (George) Morello would be just another of the hundreds of Chicago's unsolved gangland killings.

"Lost a friend of mine last night," Sam said.

"My condolences. But I don't think he was such a good friend. He loused up that job with the girl, and he tried to sell me a cemetery plot last night."

The possibility of a phone tap kept the conversation elliptical; but we were right on track with each other.

"In other words," Sam said, "you only did what you had to do."

"That's right."

"What about that item you were gonna try to obtain for me?"

"It's in the hands of the U.S. Postal Service right now. Sealed tight—marked personal. I sent it to you at your liquor store on the West Side."

"That was prompt. You just got hold of the thing last night, right?"

"Right. No time to make copies. I didn't *want* a copy, Sam. Your business is your business. Anything I can do to make your happy home stay that way is fine with me. I got a wife, too. I understand these things."

There was a long, long pause.

Then: "I'll put your check in the mail, Heller. Pleasure doin' business with you."

"Always glad to hear from a satisfied customer."

There was a briefer pause.

"You wouldn't want to go on a yearly retainer, would you, Heller?"

"No thanks, Sam. I do appreciate it. Like to stay on your good side."

"That's wise, Heller. Sorry you had that trouble last night. Wasn't my doing."

"I know, Sam."

"You done good work. You done me a favor, really. If I can pay you back, you know the number."

"Thanks, Sam. That check you mentioned is plenty, though."

"Hey, and nice going on that other thing. That sex-maniac guy. Showed the cops up. Congratulations, war hero."

The phone clicked dead.

I swallowed and sat there at my desk, trembling.

While I had no desire to work for Sam Flood ever again, I did truly want to stay on his good side. And I had made no mention of what I knew was a key factor in his wanting that photo back.

It had little, if anything, to do with keeping his wife from seeing him pictured with his former girl friend: it was the table of Sam's friends, glimpsed behind Sam and the girl in the photo. Top mobsters from Chicago, New York, Cleveland and Detroit. Some kind of informal underworld summit meeting had been inadvertently captured by a nightclub photographer. Proof of a nationwide alliance of organized crime families, perhaps in a major meeting to discuss post-war plans.

If Sam suspected that I knew the true significance of that photo, I might not live to see my kid come into the world.

And I really wanted to.

19

A little over a week later, I was having lunch at Binyon's with Ken Levine, the attorney who had brought Bob Keenan and me together. The restaurant was a businessman's bastion, wooden booths, spartan decor; my old office was around the corner, but for years I'd been only an occasional customer here. Now that business was good, and my suits were Brooks Brothers not Maxwell Street, I could afford to hobnob on a more regular basis with the brokers, lawyers and other well-to-do thieves.

"You couldn't ask for better publicity," Ken said. He was a small handsome man with sharp dark eyes that didn't miss anything and a hairline that was a memory.

"I'm taking on two more operatives," I said, sipping my rum cocktail.

"That's great. Glad it's working out so well for you." He made a clicking sound in his cheek. "Of course, the Bar Association may have something to say about the way that Lapps kid has been mistreated by Chicago's finest."

"I could bust out crying at the thought," I said.

"Yeah, well they've questioned him under sodium pentathol, hooked his nuts up to electrodes, done all sorts of zany stuff. And then they leak these vague, inadmissible 'confessions' to the papers. These wild stories of 'George' doing the crimes."

Nobody had connected George Morello to the case. Except me, of course, and I wasn't talking.

"The kid faked a coma for days," I said, "and then claimed amnesia. They had to do something."

Ken smiled wryly. "Nate, they brought in a priest and read last rites over him, to try to trick him into a 'death-bed' confession. They didn't feed him any solid food for four days. They held him six days without charging him or letting him talk to a lawyer. They probably beat the shit out of him, too."

I shrugged, sipped my cocktail. It was my second.

"Only it may backfire on 'em," Ken said. "All this dual personality stuff has the makings of an insanity plea. He's got some weird sexual deviation—his burglaries were sexually based, you know."

"How do you mean?"

"He got some kind of thrill out of entering the window of a strange apartment. He'd have a sexual emission shortly after entering. Must've been symbolic in his mind—entering through the window for him was like . . . you know." He shrugged. "Apparently the kid's never had normal sex."

"Thank you, Dr. Freud."

Ken grinned. "Hey, I could get that little bastard off."

I was glad it wasn't Ken's case.

"Whatever his sex quirk," I said, "they tied him to the assault on that nurse, Katherine Reynolds. They matched his prints to one left in her apartment. And to a partial print on the Keenan kidnap note."

"The key word is partial," Ken said, raising a finger. "They got six points of similarity on the note. Eleven are required for a positive I.D."

"They've got an *eye witness* I.D."

Ken laughed; there was genuine mirth in it. Lawyers can find the humor in both abstract thinking and human suffering. "Their eye witness is that old German janitor who was their best suspect till you nabbed Lapps. The old boy looked at four overweight, middle-aged cops and one seventeen-year-old in a line-up and somehow managed to pick out the seventeen-year-old. Before that, his description of the guy he saw was limited to 'a man in a brown raincoat with a shopping bag.' Did you know that that janitor used to be a butcher?"

"There was something in the papers about it. That doesn't mean he cuts up little girls."

"No. But if he lost his job during the war, 'cause of OPA restrictions, he could bear Bob Keenan a grudge."

"Bob wasn't with the OPA long enough for that to be possible. He was with the New York office. Jesus, Ken, what's your point, here?"

Like most attorneys, Ken was argumentative for the sheer hell of it; but he saw this was getting under my skin and backed off. "Just making conversation, Nate. That kid's guilty. The prosecutors are just goddamn lucky they got a mean little j.d. who carried Nietzsche around and collected

Nazi memorabilia. 'Cause without public opinion, they couldn't win this one."

Ken headed back to court and I sat working at my cocktail, wondering if I could get away with a third.

I shared some of Ken's misgivings about the way the Lapps case was being handled. A handwriting expert had linked the lipstick message on the late Margaret Johnson's wall with that of the Keenan kidnap note; then matched those to re-creations of both which Lapps was made to give.

This handwriting expert's claim to fame was the Lindbergh case—having been there, I knew the Lindbergh handwriting evidence was a crock—and both the lipstick message and kidnap notes were printed, which made handwriting comparison close to worthless.

Of course, Lapps had misspelled some of the same words as in the note: "waite" and "safty." Only I'd learned in passing from Lieutenant Kruger that Lapps had been told to copy the notes, mistakes and all.

A fellow named Bruno Hauptmann had dutifully done the same in his handwriting samples, some years before. The line-up trick Ken had mentioned had been used to hand Hauptmann on a platter to a weak, elderly eyewitness, too. And the press had played their role in Bruno's railroading— one overeager reporter had written an incriminating phone number inside Hauptmann's apartment, to buy a headline that day, and that little piece of creative writing on wainscoting became an unrefuted key prosecution exhibit.

But so what? Bruno was (a) innocent and (b) long-dead. This kid was alive, well and psycho—and as guilty as the Nazi creeps he idolized. Besides which, what Ken had said about the kid's sexual deviation had made something suddenly clear to me.

I knew Lapps was into burglary for kicks, but I figured it was the violence against women that got him going. This business about strange buildings—and he'd had a certain type of building, hadn't he, like some guys liked blondes or other guys were leg men—made a screwy sort of sense.

Lapps must have been out on the fire escape, peeking into Caroline Williams' apartment, casing it for a possible break-in, when he saw George slapping the girl around in the bedroom. He must have heard the Williams woman calling George by name—that planted the "George did it" seed—and got a new thrill when he witnessed George cut the woman's throat.

Then George had seen the dark, cop-like figure out the window, got spooked and lammed; and Lapps entered the apartment, spilled his seed, did his sick, guilty number washing and bandaging the corpse, and took various mementos, including undies and the photo album.

This new thrill had inspired Lapps to greater heights of madness, and the second girl—Margaret Johnson—had been all his. All his own twisted handiwork . . . though perhaps in his mind George had done that, as well.

But Lapps, like so many men after even a normal sexual release, felt a sadness and even guilt and had left that lipstick plea on the wall.

That pretty nurse, Katherine Reynolds, had been lucky. Lapps hadn't been able to kill again; he'd stopped at assault—maybe he'd had his sexual release already, and his remorse kicked in before he could kill her. He'd even come back to help her.

What was bothering me, though, was the Keenan child. Nothing about Lapps' M.O. fit this crime. The building wasn't his "type." Kidnapping wasn't this crime, let alone dismembering a child. Had Lapps' thrill-seeking escalated into sheer depravity?

Even so, one thing was so wrong I couldn't invent any justification for it. Ken had said it: the kid had probably never had normal sex. The kid's idea of a fun date was going through a strange window and coming on the floor.

But rape had been attempted on the little girl. The coroner said so. Rape.

"Want some company, Heller?"

Hal Davis, with his oversize head and sideways smile, had already slid in across from me in the booth.

"Sure. What's new in the world of yellow journalism?"

"Slow day. Jeez, Heller, you look like shit."

"Thanks, Hal."

"You should be on top of the world. You're a local hero. A celebrity."

"Shut up, Hal."

Davis had brought a Scotch along with him. "Ain't this case a pip. Too bad they can't fry this kid, but in this enlightened day and age, he'll probably get a padded cell and three squares for the rest of his miserable life."

"I don't think they'll fry a seventeen-year-old, even in a case like this."

"What a case it's been. For you, especially."

"You got your share of mileage out of it, too, Hal."

He laughed; lit up a cigarette. Shook his head. "Funny."

"What is?"

"Who'd a thunk it?"

"Thunk what?"

He leaned over conspiratorially. His breath was evidence that this was not his first Scotch of the afternoon. "That the Keenan kidnapper really would turn out to be the Lipstick Killer. For real."

"Why not? He left his signature on Keenan's back fence. 'Stop me before I kill more . . .'"

"That's the funny part." He snorted smugly. "Who do you think wrote that on the fence?"

I blinked. "What do you mean?"

Davis leaned across with a one-sided smirk that split his boyish face. "Don't be a jerk. Don't be so gullible. *I* wrote that there. It made for a hell of a byline."

I grabbed him by his lapels and dragged him across the table. His Scotch spilled and my drink went over and his cigarette went flying and his eyes were wide, as were those of the businessmen finishing up their two- and three-martini lunches.

"You *what?*" I asked him through my teeth.

"Nate! You're hurting me! Let go! You're makin' a scene."

I shoved him back against the booth. I got out. I was shaking. "You did do it, didn't you, you little cocksucker."

He was frightened, but he tried not to show it; he made a face, shrugged. "What's the big fucking deal?"

I grabbed him by the tie and he watched my fist while I decided whether to smash in his face.

Then the fist dissolved into fingers, but I retained my grip on his tie.

"Let's go talk to the cops," I said.

"I was just bullshitting," he said, lamely. "I didn't do it. Really. It was just the booze talking."

I put a hand around his throat and started to squeeze. His eyes popped. I was sneering at him when I said, "Stop me, Hal—before I kill more."

Then I shoved him against the wall, rattling some framed pictures, and got the hell out of there.

20

The cellar was lit by a single hanging bulb. There were laundry tubs and storage lockers, just like the basement where JoAnn Keenan was dismembered.

But this was not that basement. This was a slightly smaller one in a building near the "murder cellar," a tidy one with tools and cleaning implements neatly lining the walls, like well-behaved prisoners.

This was janitor Otto Bergstrum's domain.

"Why you want meet with me?" the thick-necked, white-haired Bergstrum asked.

Outside, it was rainy and dark. Close to midnight. I was in a drenched trenchcoat, getting Bergstrum's tidy cellar damp. I left my hat on and it was dripping, too.

"I told you on the phone," I said. "Business. A matter of money."

As before, the husky old fellow was in coveralls, his biceps tight against the rolled-up sleeves of his flannel shirt; his legs were planted well apart and firmly. His hands were fists and the fists were heavily veined.

"You come about reward money," he said. His eyes were blue and unblinking and cold under unruly salt-and-pepper eyebrows. "You try talk me out of claim my share."

"That's not it exactly. You see, there's going to be several people put in claims."

"Cops not eligible."

"Just city cops. I'm eligible."

"But they not."

"Right. But I have to kick back a few bucks to a couple of 'em, out of what I haul to shore."

"So, what? You think I should help you pay them?"

"No. I think you should kick your share back to me."

His eyes flared; he took a step forward. We were still a number of paces apart, though. Christ, his arms and shoulders were massive.

"Why should I do this?"

"Because I think you kidnapped the Keenan girl," I said.

He took a step back. His mouth dropped open. His eyes widened.

"I'm in clear," he said.

That was less than a denial, wasn't it?

"Otto," I said, "I checked up on you, this afternoon. Discreetly. You're a veteran, like me—only you served in the first war. On the other side."

He jutted his jaw. "I am proud to be German."

"But you were an American immigrant at the time. You'd been in this country since you were a kid. But still you went back home, to fight for the fatherland . . . then after they lost their asses, you had the nerve to come back."

"I was not alone in doing such."

He wasn't, either: on the North Side, there was a whole organization of these German World War One vets who got together. They even had dinners with American vets.

"The Butcher's Union knew about you," I said, "but you were never a member."

"Communists," he said.

"You worked as a butcher in a shop on the West Side, for years—till meat shortages during the war. . . this *last* war . . . got you laid off. You were non-union, couldn't find another butcher job . . . with your background, anything defense-related was out. You wound up here. A janitor. It's your sister's building, isn't it?"

"You go to hell, mister."

"You know what I think, Otto? I think you blamed the New

Deal for your bad deal. I think you got real mad at the government. I think you in particular blamed the OPA."

"Socialists," he said.

"Bob Keenan wasn't even in Chicago when you got laid off, you stupid old fart. But he was in the OPA now, and he was in the neighborhood. He had money, and he had a pretty little daughter. He was as good a place as any for Otto Bergstrum to get even."

"There is no proof of any of this. It is all air. Wind. You are the fart."

"What, did you get drunk, was it spur of the moment, or did you plan it? The kidnapping I can see. What I don't understand is killing the little girl. Did she start to make noise in bed, and you strangled her? Were you just too strong, and maybe drunk, and it was an accident of sorts?"

Now his face was an expressionless mask. His hands weren't fists any more. His eyes were hooded; his head was slack.

"What I really don't get, Otto, is the rape. Trying to rape a little girl. Was she already dead? You sick fucker."

He raised his head. "You have filthy mouth. Maybe I wash it out with lye."

"I'm going to give you a choice, old man. You can come with me, and come clean at Summerdale station. Or I can kill you right here."

"You have gun in your coat pocket?"

"I have gun in my coat pocket, yeah."

"Ah. But my friend has knife."

I hadn't heard him. I have no idea where he came from; coal bin, maybe. He was as quiet as nobody there. He was just suddenly behind me and he did have a knife, a long, sharp butcher knife that caught the single bulb's glow and reflected it, like the glint of a madman's eyes. Like the glint of this madman's eyes, as I stepped quickly to one side, the knife slashing down, cutting through the arm of my raincoat, cutting cloth and ripping a wound along my shoulder. My hand involuntarily released the gun, and even though both it and my hand were in the same coat pocket, I was fumbling for it, the gun caught in the cloth, my fingers searching for the grip. . . .

I recognized this rail-thin, shorthaired, sunken-cheeked young man as James Watson—but only from the papers. I'd never met him. He was the handyman at the nursery from which the kidnap ladder had been "stolen"; an Army vet and an accused child molester and, with Otto, a suspect in this case till I hauled Jerome Lapps onstage.

He was wearing a rain slicker, yellow, and one of those floppy yellow wide-brimmed rain hats; but he didn't look like he'd been outside. Maybe his raincoat was to keep the blood off.

He had the knife raised in such a corny fashion; raised in one fist, level with his head, and walking mummy-slow. His dark-blue eyes were wide and his grin glazed and he looked silly, like a scarecrow with a knife, a caricature of a fiend. I could have laughed at how hokey this asshole looked, only Otto had grabbed me from behind as Watson advanced.

With my arms pulled back, one of them bleeding and burning from the slash of a knife that was even now red with my blood, I struggled but with little success. The old German janitor had me locked in his thick hands.

Watson stabbed savagely with the knife and I moved to the left and the blade, about half of it, went into Otto's neck and blood spurted. Otto went down, clutching his throat, his life oozing through his fingers, and I was free of him, and while Watson still had the knife in his hand—he'd withdrawn the blade almost as quickly as he'd accidentally sunk it into his cohort's throat—the handyman was stunned by the turn of events, his mouth hanging open, as if awaiting a dentist's drill. I grabbed his wrist with my two hands and swung his hand and his knife in a sudden arc down into his stomach.

The sound was like sticking your foot in thick mud.

He stood there, doing the oddest little dance, for several seconds, his hand gripped around the handle of the butcher knife, which I had driven in almost to the hilt. He looked down at himself with a look of infinite stupidity and danced some more.

I pushed his stupid face with the heel of my hand and he went ass-over-tea-kettle. He lay on his back twitching. He'd released the knife. I yanked the knife out of his stomach; there was a slit in the rain slicker where the knife went in.

And the sound was like pulling your foot out of thick mud.

"You're the one who tried to rape that little girl, aren't you, Jim?"

He was blinking and twitching; a thin geyser of blood was coming from the slit in the yellow rain slicker.

"Poor old Otto just wanted to get even. Pull a little kidnap, make a little money off those socialist sons of bitches who cost him his job. But he picked a bad assistant in you, Jim. Had to play butcher on that dead little girl, trying to clean up after you."

There was still life in Watson's eyes. Otto was over near the laundry tubs, gurgling. Alive, barely.

I had the knife in one hand, and my blood was soaking my shirt under the raincoat, though I felt little if any pain. I gave some serious thought to whaling away on Watson with the butcher knife; just carving the fucker up. But I couldn't quite cross the line.

I had George Morello's pack of Camels in my suitcoat pocket. I dug them out and smoked while I watched both men die.

Better part of two cigarettes, it took.

Then I wiped off anything I'd touched, dropped the butcher knife near Watson, and left that charnel house behind; went out into a dark, warm summer night and a warm, cleansing summer rain, which put out the second cigarette.

It was down to the butt, anyway. I tossed it in a sewer.

2 1

The deaths of Otto Bergstrum and James Watson made a bizarre sidebar in the ongoing saga of the Lipstick Killer, but neither the cops nor the press allowed the "fatal falling out between friends" to influence the accepted scenario.

It turned out there was even something of a motive: Watson had loaned Otto five hundred dollars to pay off a gambling debt; Otto played the horses, it seemed. Speculation was that Watson, knowing Otto was due reward money from the Keenan case, had demanded payment. Both men were known to have bad tempers. Both had killed in the war—well, each in his individual war.

The cops never figured out how the two men had managed to kill each other with the one knife, not that anybody seemed to care. It was fine with me. Nobody had seen me in the vicinity that rainy night, or at least nobody who bothered to report it.

Lapps was indicted on multiple burglary, assault, and murder charges. His lawyers entered into what years later an investigative journalist would term "a strange, unprecedented cooperative relationship" with the State's Attorney's office.

In order to save their client from the electric chair, the defense lawyers—despite the prosecution's admission of the "small likelihood of a successful murder prosecution of Jerome Lapps"—advised the boy to cop a plea.

If Lapps were to confess to the murders of Caroline Williams, Margaret Johnson and JoAnn Keenan, the State's Attorney would seek concurrent life sentences. That meant parole in twenty years.

Lapps—reluctantly, I'm told—accepted the plea bargain, but when the boy was taken into a judge's presence to make a formal admission of guilt, he said instead, "I don't remember killing anybody."

The recantation cost him. Even though Lapps eventually gave everybody the confession they wanted, the deal was off: all he got out of it was avoiding the chair. His three life terms were concurrent with a recommendation of no parole. Ever.

He tried to hang himself in his cell, but it didn't take.

I took a ride on the Rock Island Rocket to Joliet to visit Lapps, about a year after he was sent up.

The visiting room at Stateville was a long narrow room cut in half by a long wide table with a glass divider. I'd already taken my seat with the other visitors when guards paraded in a handful of prisoners.

Lapps, like the others, wore blue denims and a blue-and-white striped shirt, which looked like a normal dress shirt, unless the wearer turned to reveal a stenciled number across the back. The husky, good-looking kid had changed little in appearance; maybe he was a little heavier. His dark, wavy hair, though no shorter, was cut differently—it was neater looking, a student's hair, not a j.d.'s.

He sat and smiled shyly. "I remember you."

"You should. You tried to shoot me."

"That's what I understand. I'm sorry."

"You don't remember?"

"No."

"The gun you used was one you'd stolen. The owner identified it along with other stuff of his you took."

He shrugged; this was all news to him.

I continued: "The owner said the gun had been his father's and had been stuck in a drawer for seventeen years. Hadn't been fired for a long time."

His brow knit. "That's why the gun didn't go off, when I shot at you?"

"Yes. But a ballistics expert said the third shot *would* have gone off. You'd reactivated the trigger."

"I'm glad it didn't."

"Me too."

We looked at each other. My gaze was hard, unforgiving; his was evasive, shy.

"Why are you here, Mr. Heller?"

"I wanted to ask you a question. Why did you confess to all three murders?"

He shrugged again. "I had to. Otherwise, I'd be dead, my lawyers say. I just made things up. Told them what they wanted to hear. Repeated things back to them. Used what I read in the papers." One more shrug. Then his dark eyes tightened. "Why? You asked me like . . . like you knew I didn't do them."

"You did one of them, Jerry. You killed Margaret Williams and you wrote that lipstick message on her wall."

Something flickered in his eyes. "I don't remember."

"Maybe not. But you also assaulted Katherine Reynolds,

and you tried to shoot me. As far as I'm concerned, that's why you're here."

"You don't think I killed that little girl?"

"I know you didn't."

An eagerness sprang into his passive face. "Have you talked to my lawyers?"

I shook my head no.

"Would you talk to my . . ."

"No. I'm not going to help you, Jerry."

"Why . . . why are you telling me this, then . . . ?"

My voice was barely above a whisper; this was just between us guys. "In case you're not faking. In case you really don't remember what you did. I think you got a right to know what you're doing time for. What you're really doing time for. And you did kill the second girl. And you almost killed the nurse. And you damn near killed me. That's why you're here, Jerry. That's why I'm leaving you here to rot, and don't bother repeating what I'm telling you, because I can out-lie every con in Stateville. I used to be a Chicago cop."

He was reeling. "Who . . . who killed the first girl? Who killed that Caroline Williams lady?"

"Jerry," I said, rising to go, "George did it."

2 2

Lapps, as of this writing, is still inside. That's why, after all these years, as I edge toward senility in my Coral Springs condo, in the company of my second wife, I have put all this down on paper. The Parole for Lapps Committee requested a formal deposition, but I preferred that this take the same form, more or less, as other memoirs I've scribbled in my dotage.

Jerry Lapps is an old man now—not as old as me, but old. A gray-haired, paunchy old boy. Not the greasy-haired j.d. who I was glad to see go to hell and Stateville. He's been in custody longer than any other inmate in the Illinois prison system. Long before courses were offered to prisoners, he was the first Illinois inmate to earn a college degree. He then helped and advised other convicts with organizing similar self-help correspondence-course programs. He taught himself electronics and became a pretty fair watercolor artist. Right now he's in Vienna prison, a minimum-security facility with no fences and no barred windows. He's the assistant to the prison chaplain.

Over the years, the press and public servants and surviving relatives of the murder victims—including JoAnn's sister Jane—have fought Lapps' parole. He is portrayed as the first of a particular breed of American urban monster—precursor to Richard Speck, John Wayne Gacy and Ted Bundy.

Bob Keenan died last year. His wife Norma died three years ago.

Sam Flood—a.k.a. Sam Giancana—was hit in his home back in '75, right before he was supposed to testify before a Senate committee about Outfit/CIA connections.

Of the major players, Lapps is the only one left alive. Lapps and me.

What the hell. I've had my fill of revenge.

Let the bastard loose.

If he's faking rehabilitation like he once faked amnesia, if he hurts anybody else, shit—I'll haul the nine millimeter out of mothballs and hobble after him myself.

23

My son was born just before midnight, on September 27, 1947.

We named him Nathan Samuel Heller, Jr.

His mother—exhausted after twelve hours of labor, face slick with sweat, hair matted down—never looked more beautiful to me. And I never saw her look happier.

"He's so small," she said. "Why did he take so long making his entrance?"

"He's small but he's stubborn. Like his mother."

"He's got your nose. He's got your mouth. He's gorgeous. You want to hold him, Nate?"

"Sure."

I took the little bundle, and looked at the sweet small face and experienced, for the first and only time before or since, love at first sight.

"I'm Daddy," I told the groggy little fellow. He made saliva bubbles. I touched his tiny nose. Examined his tiny hand—the miniature palm, the perfect little fingers. How could something so miraculous happen in such an awful world?

I gave him back to his mother and she put him to her breast and he began to suckle. A few minutes on the planet, and he was getting tit already. Life wasn't going to get much better.

I sat there and watched them and waves of joy and sadness alternated over me. It was mostly joy, but I couldn't keep from thinking that a hopeful mother had once held a tiny child named JoAnn in her arms, minutes after delivery; that another mother had held little Jerry Lapps in her gentle grasp. And Caroline Williams and Margaret Johnson were once babes in their mother's arms. One presumes even Otto Bergstrum and

James Watson and, Christ, George Morello were sweet infants in their sweet mother's arms, once upon a time.

I promised myself that my son would have it better than me. He wouldn't have to have it so goddamn rough; the depression was ancient history, and the war to end all wars was over. He'd want for nothing. Food, clothing, shelter, education, they were his birthright.

That's what we'd fought for, all of us. To give our kids what we never had. To give them a better, safer place to live in. Life, liberty and the pursuit of happiness.

For that one night, settled into a hard hospital chair, in the glow of my brand-new little family, I allowed myself to believe that that hope was not a vain one. That anything was possible in this glorious post-war world.

PRIVATE CONSULTATION

I GRABBED THE LAKE STREET EL AND GOT off at Garfield Park; it was a short walk from there to the "Death Clinic" at 3406 West Monroe Street. That's what the papers, some of them anyway, were calling the Wynekoop mansion. To me it was just another big old stone building on the West Side, one of many, though of a burnt-reddish stone rather than typical Chicago gray. And, I'll grant you, the three-story structure was planted on a wealthier residential stretch than the one I'd grown up on, twelve blocks south.

Still, this was the West Side, and more or less my old stomping grounds, and that was no doubt part of why I'd been asked to drop by the Wynekoop place this sunny Saturday afternoon. The family had most likely asked around, heard about the ex-cop from nearby Douglas Park who now had a little private agency in the Loop.

And my reputation on the West Side—and in the Loop— was of being just honest enough, and just crooked enough, to get most jobs done.

But part of why I'd been called, I would guess, was Earle

Wynekoop himself. I knew Earle a little, from a distance. We'd both worked at the World's Fair down on the lakefront last summer and fall. I was working pickpocket duty, and Earle was in the front office, doing whatever front-office people do. We were both about the same age—I was twenty-seven—but he seemed like a kid to me.

Earle mostly chased skirts, except at the Streets of Paris exhibition, where the girls didn't wear skirts. Tall, handsome, wavy-haired Earle, with his white teeth and pencil-line mustache, had pursued the fan dancers with the eagerness of a plucked bird trying to get its feathers back.

Funny thing was, nobody—including me—knew Earle was a married man, till November, when the papers were full of his wife. His wife's murder, that is.

Now it was a sunny, almost-warm afternoon in December, and I had been in business just under a year. And like most small businessmen, I'd had less than a prosperous 1933. A retainer from a family with the Wynekoop's dough would be a nice way to ring out the old and ring in the new.

Right now, I was ringing the doorbell. I was up at the top of the first-floor landing; Dr. Alice Wynekoop's office was in an English basement below. I was expecting a maid or butler to answer, considering the size of this place. But Earle is what I got.

His white smile flickered nervously. He adjusted his bow tie with one hand and offered the other for me to shake, which I did. His grip was weak and moist, like his dark eyes.

"Mr. Heller," he said. "Thank you for stopping by."

"My pleasure," I said, stepping into the vestibule, hat in hand.

Earle, snappily dressed in a pinstripe worsted, took my topcoat and hung it on a hall tree.

"Perhaps you don't remember me," he said. "I worked in the

front office at the fair this summer."

"Sure I remember you, Mr. Wynekoop."

"Why don't you call me 'Earle.'"

"Fine, Earle," I said. "And my friends call me 'Nate.'"

He grinned nervously and said, "Step into the library, Nate, if you would."

"Is your mother here?"

"No. She's in jail."

"Why haven't you sprung her?" Surely these folks could afford to make bail. On the phone, Earle had quickly agreed to my rate of fifteen bucks a day and one-hundred-dollar non-refundable retainer. And that was the top of my sliding scale.

An eyebrow arched in disgust on a high, unwrinkled brow. "Mother is ill, thanks to these barbarians. We've decided to let the state pay for her illness, considering they've provoked it."

He tried to sound indignant through all that, but petulance was the result.

The interior of the house was on the gloomy side; a lot of dark, expensive, well-wrought woodwork, and heavy, plush furnishings that dated back to the turn of the century, when the house was built. There were hints that the Wynekoops might not be as well fixed as the rest of us thought: ornate anti-quated light fixtures, worn Oriental carpets and a layer of dust indicated yesterday's wealth, not today's.

I sat on a dark horsehair couch; two of the walls were bookcases, filled with leather-bound volumes, and the others were hung with somber landscapes. The first thing Earle did was give me an envelope with one hundred dollars in tens in it. Now Earle was getting himself some sherry off a liquor cart.

"Can I get you something?" Earle asked. His hands were shaking as he poured himself the sherry.

"This will do nicely," I said, counting the money.

"Don't be a wet blanket, Nate."

I put the money-clipped bills away. "Rum, then. No ice."

He gave me a glass and sat beside me. I'd have rather he sat across from me; it was awkward, looking sideways at him. But he seemed to crave the intimacy.

"Mother's not guilty, you know."

"Really."

"I confessed, but they didn't believe me. I confessed five times."

"Cops figured you were trying to clear your mama."

"Yes. I'm afraid so. I rather botched it, as a liar."

It was good rum. "Then you didn't kill your wife?"

"Kill Rheta! Don't be silly. I loved her, once. Just because our marriage had gone . . . well, anyway, I didn't do it, and Mother didn't do it, either."

"Who did, then?"

He smirked humorlessly. "I think some moron did it. Some fool looking for narcotics and money. That's why I called you, Nate. The police aren't looking for the killer. They think they have their man in Mother."

"What does your mother's attorney think?"

"He thinks hiring an investigator is a splendid idea."

"Doesn't he have his own man?"

"Yes, but I wanted you. I remembered you from the fair . . . and, I asked around."

What did I tell you? Am I a detective?

"I can't promise I can clear her," I said. "She confessed, after all—and the cops took her one confession more seriously than your five."

"They gave her the third-degree. A sixty-three-year-old woman! Respected in the community! Can you imagine?"

"Who was the cop in charge?"

Earle pursed his lips in disgust. "Captain Stege himself, the bastard."

"Is this *his* case? Damn."

"Yes, it's Stege's case. Didn't you read about all this in the papers?"

"Sure I did. But I didn't read it like I thought I was going to be involved. I probably did read Stege was in charge, but when you called this morning, I didn't recall . . ."

"Why, Nate? Is this a problem?"

"No," I lied.

I let it go at that, as I needed the work, but the truth was, Stege hated my guts. I'd testified against a couple of cops, which Stege—even though he was honest and those two cops were bent even by Chicago standards—took as a betrayal of the police brotherhood.

Earle was up pouring himself another sherry. Already. "Mother is a sensitive, frail woman, with a heart condition, and she was ruthlessly, mercilessly questioned for a period of over twenty-four hours."

"I see."

"I'm afraid . . ." And Earle sipped his sherry greedily. Swallowed. Continued: "I'm afraid I may have made the situation even worse."

"How?"

He sat again, sighed, shrugged. "As you probably know, I was out of town when Rheta was . . . slain."

That was an odd choice of words; "slain" was something nobody said, a word in the newspapers, not real life.

"I went right to the Fillmore police station, when I returned from Kansas City. I had a moment with mother. I said . . ." He slumped, shook his head.

"Go on, Earle."

"I said . . . God help me, I said, 'For God's sake, Mother, if you did this on account of me, go ahead and confess.'" He touched his fingertips to his eyes.

"What did she say to you?"

"She . . . she said, 'Earle, I did not kill Rheta.' But then she went in for another round with Captain Stege, and . . ."

"And made that cockamamie confession she later retracted."

"Yes."

"Why did you think your mother might have killed your wife for you, Earle?"

"Because . . . because Mother loves me very much."

Dr. Alice Lindsay Wynekoop had been one of Chicago's most esteemed female physicians for almost four decades. She had met her late husband Frank in medical college, and with him continued the Wynekoop tradition of care for the ill and disabled. Her charity work in hospitals and clinics was well known; a prominent clubwoman, a humanitarian, a leader in the woman's suffrage movement, Dr. Wynekoop was an unlikely candidate for a murder charge.

But she had indeed been charged: with the murder of her daughter-in-law, in the basement consultation office in this very house.

Earle led me there, down a narrow stairway off the dining room. In the central basement hallway were two facing doors: Dr. Wynekoop's office, at left; and at right, an examination room. The door was open. Earle motioned for me to go in, which I did, but he stayed in the doorway.

The room was narrow and wide and cold; the steam heat was off. The dominant fixture was an old-fashioned, brown, leather-covered examination table. A chair under a large stained-glass window, whose ledge was lined with medical books, sat next to a weigh-and-measure scale. In one corner was a medicine and instrument cabinet.

"The police wouldn't let us clean up properly," Earle said.

The leather exam table was bloodstained.

"They said they might take the whole damn table in," Earle

said. "And use it in court, for evidence."

I nodded. "What about your mother's office? She claimed burglary."

"Well, yes . . . some drugs were taken from the cabinet, in here. And six dollars from a drawer . . ."

He led me across the hall to an orderly office area with a big rolltop desk, which he pointed to.

"And," Earle said, pulling open a middle drawer, "there was the gun, of course. Taken from here."

"The cops found it across the hall, though. By the body."

"Yes," Earle said, quietly.

"Tell me about her, Earle."

"Mother?"

"Rheta."

"She . . . she was a lovely girl. A beautiful redhead. Gifted musician . . . violinist. But she was . . . sick."

"Sick how?"

He tapped his head. "She was a hypochondriac. Imagining she had this disease, and that one. Her mother died of tuberculosis . . . in an insane asylum, no less. Rheta came to imagine she had t.b., like her mother. What they did have in common, I'm afraid, was being mentally deranged."

"You said you loved her, Earle."

"I did. Once. The marriage was a failure. I . . . I had to seek affection elsewhere." A wicked smile flickered under the pencil mustache. "I've never had trouble finding women, Nate. I have a little black book with fifty girlfriends in it."

It occurred to me that a real man could get by on a considerably shorter list; but I keep opinions like that to myself, when given a hundred-buck retainer.

"What did the little woman think about all these girlfriends? A crowd like that is hard to hide."

He shrugged. "We never talked about it."

"No talk of a divorce?"

He licked his lips, avoided my eyes. "I wanted one, Nate. She wouldn't give it to me. A good Catholic girl."

Four of the most frightening words in the English language, to any healthy male anyway.

"The two of you lived here, with your mother?"

"Yes . . . I can't really afford to live elsewhere. Times are hard, you know."

"So I hear. Who else lives here? Isn't there a roomer?"

"Yes. Miss Shaunesey. She's a high school teacher."

"Is she here now?"

"Yes. I asked if she'd talk to you, and she is more than willing. Anything to help Mother."

Back in the library, I sat and spoke with Miss Enid Shaunesey, a prim, slim woman of about fifty. Earle lurked in the background, helping himself to more sherry.

"What happened that day, Miss Shaunesey?"

November 21, 1933.

"I probably arose at about a quarter to seven," she said, with a little shrug, adjusting her wire-frame glasses. "I had breakfast in the house with Dr. Alice. I don't remember whether Rheta had breakfast with us or not . . . I don't really remember speaking to Rheta at all that morning."

"Then you went on to school?"

"Yes," she said. "I teach at Marshall High. I completed my teaching duties and signed out about three-fifteen. I went to the Loop and shopped until a little after five and went home."

"What, at about six?"

"Or a little after. When I came home, Dr. Alice was in the kitchen, preparing dinner. She fried up some pork chops. Made a nice salad, cabbage, potatoes, peaches. It was just the two of us. We're good friends."

"Earle was out of town, of course, but what about Rheta?"

"She was supposed to dine with us, but she was late. We went ahead without her. I didn't think much of it. The girl had a mind of her own; she frequently went here and there—music lessons, shopping." There was a faint note of disapproval, though the conduct she was describing mirrored her own after-school activities of that same day.

"Did Dr. Wynekoop seem to get along with Rheta?"

"They had their tiffs, but Dr. Alice loved the girl. She was family. That evening, during dinner, she spoke of Rheta, in fact."

"What did she say?"

"She was worried about the girl."

"Because she hadn't shown up for supper?"

"Yes, and after the meal she telephoned a neighbor or two, to see if they'd seen Rheta. But she also expressed a more general concern—Rheta was fretting about her health, you see. As I said, Rheta frequently stayed out. We knew she'd probably gone into the Loop to shop and, as she often did, she probably went to a motion picture. That was what we thought."

"I see."

Miss Shaunesey sat up, her expression suddenly thoughtful. "Of course, I'd noticed Rheta's coat and hat on the table here in the library, but Dr. Alice said that she'd probably worn her good coat and hat to the Loop. Anyway, after dinner we talked, and then I went to the drugstore for Dr. Alice, to have a prescription refilled."

"When did you get back?"

"Well, you see, the drugstore is situated at Madison and Kedzie. That store did not have as many tablets as Dr. Alice wanted, so I walked to the drugstore at Homan and Madison and got a full bottle."

"So it took a while," I said, trying not to get irritated with her fussy old-maid-schoolteacher thoroughness. It beat the hell out of an uncooperative, unobservant witness, though. I guessed.

"I was home by half past seven, I should judge. Then we sat down in the library and talked for about an hour. We discussed two books—*Strange Interlude* was one and the other was *The Forsythe Saga.*"

"Did Dr. Wynekoop seem relaxed, or was she in any way preoccupied?"

"The former," Miss Shaunesey said with certainty. "Any concern about Rheta's absence was strictly routine."

"At what point did Dr. Wynekoop go downstairs to her consultation room?"

"Well, I was complaining of my hyperacidity. Dr. Alice said she had something in her office that she thought I could use for that. It was in a glass case in her consulting room. Of course, she never got that medicine for me."

Dr. Wynekoop had been interrupted in her errand by the discovery of the body of her daughter-in-law Rheta. The corpse was face down on the examination table, head up on a white pillow. Naked, the body was wrapped in a sheet and a blanket, snugged in around the feet and pulled up over the shoulders, like a child lovingly tucked into bed. Rheta had been shot, once, in the back. Her lips were scorched as if by acid. A wet towel was under her mouth, indicating perhaps that chloroform had been administered. A half-empty bottle of chloroform was found on the washstand. And a gauze-wrapped .32 Smith and Wesson rested on the pillow above the girl's head.

"Dr. Wynekoop did not call the police?" I asked, knowing the answer. This much I remembered from the papers.

"No."

"Or an undertaker, or the coroner's office?"

"No. She called her daughter, Catherine."

Earle looked up from his sherry long enough to interject: "Catherine is a doctor, too. She's a resident at the Children's Department at Cook County Hospital."

And that was my logical first stop. I took the El over to the hospital, a block-square graystone at Harrison and Ogden; this job was strictly a West Side affair.

Dr. Catherine Wynekoop was a beautiful woman. Her dark hair was pulled back from her pale, pretty face; in her doctor's whites, she sat in the hospital cafeteria stirring her coffee as we spoke.

"I was on duty here when Mother called," she said. "She said, 'Something terrible has happened at home . . . it's Rheta . . . she's dead . . . she has been shot.'"

"How did she sound? Hysterical? Calm?"

"Calm, but a shocked sort of calm." She sighed. "I went home immediately. Mother seemed all right, but I noticed her gait was a little unsteady. Her hands were trembling, her face was flushed. I helped her to a chair in the dining room and rushed out in the kitchen for stimuli. I put a teaspoonful of aromatic spirits of ammonia in water and had her drink it."

"She hadn't called anyone but you, as yet?"

"No. She said she'd just groped her way up the stairs, that on the way everything went black, she felt dizzy, that the next thing she knew she was at the telephone calling me."

"Did you take charge, then?"

A half-smile twitched at her cheek. "I guess I did. I called Mr. Ahearn."

"Mr. Ahearn?"

"The undertaker. And I called Dr. Berger, our family physician."

"You really should have called the coroner."

"Mother later said that she'd asked me to, on the phone, but I didn't hear that or understand her or something. We were

upset. Once Dr. Berger and Mr. Ahearn arrived, the coroner's
office was called."

She kept stirring her coffee, staring into it.

"How did you and Rheta get along?"

She lifted her eyebrows in a shrug. "We weren't close. We
had little in common. But there was no animosity."

She seemed goddamn guarded to me; I decided to try and
knock her wall down, or at least jar some stones loose.

I said: "Do you think your mother killed Rheta?"

Her dark eyes rose to mine and flashed. "Of course not. I
never heard my mother speak an unkind word to or about
Rheta." She searched her mind for an example, and came up
with one: "Why—whenever mother bought me a dress, she
bought one for Rheta, also."

She returned her gaze to the coffee, which she stirred
methodically.

Then she continued: "She was worried about Rheta, actually. Worried about the way Earle was treating her. Worried
about all the . . . well, about the crowd he started to run around
with down at the World's Fair. Mother asked me to talk to him
about it."

"About what, exactly?"

"His conduct."

"You mean, his girlfriends."

She looked at me sharply. "Mr. Heller, my understanding is
that you are in our family's employ. Some of these questions
of yours seem uncalled for."

I gave her my most charming smile. "Miss Wynekoop . . .
Doctor . . . I'm like you. Sometimes I have to ask unpleasant
questions, if I'm going to make the proper diagnosis."

She considered that a moment, then smiled. It was a honey
of a smile, making mine look like the shabby sham it was.

"I understand, Mr. Heller." She rose. She'd never touched
the coffee once. "I'm afraid I have afternoon rounds to make."

She extended her hand; it was delicate, but her grasp had strength, and she had dignity. Hard to believe she was Earle's sister.

I had my own rounds to make, and at a different hospital; it took a couple of streetcars to do the job. The County Jail was a grim, low-slung graystone lurking behind the Criminal Courts Building. This complex of city buildings was just south of a West Side residential area, just eight blocks south of Douglas Park. Old home week for me.

Alice Wynekoop was sitting up in bed, reading a medical journal, when I was led to her by a matron. She was in the corner and had much of the ward to herself; the beds on either side were empty.

She was of average size, but frail-looking; she appeared much older than her sixty-three years, her flesh freckled with liver spots, her neck creped. The skin of her face had a wilted look, dark patches under the eyes, saggy jowls.

But her eyes were dark and sharp. And her mouth was a stern line.

"Are you a policeman?" she asked. Her tone was neutral.

I had my hat in hand. "I'm Nathan Heller," I said. "I'm the private investigator your son hired."

She smiled in a businesslike way, extended her hand for me to shake, which I did. Surprisingly strong for such a weak-looking woman.

"Pull up a chair, Mr. Heller," she said. Her voice was clear and crisp. Someone very different than the woman she outwardly appeared to be lived inside that worn-out body.

I sat. "I'm going to be asking around about some things . . . inquire about burglaries in your neighborhood and such."

She nodded, twice, very business-like. "I'm certain the thief was after narcotics. In fact, some narcotics were taken, but I keep precious few in my surgery."

"Yes. I see. What about the gun?"

"It was my husband's. We've had it for years. I've never fired it in my life."

I took out my small spiral notebook. "I know you're weary of telling it, but I need to hear your story. Before I go poking around the edges of this case, I need to understand the center of it."

She nodded and smiled. "What would you like to know, exactly?"

"When did you last see your daughter-in-law?"

"About three o'clock that Tuesday. She said she was going for a walk with Mrs. Donovan . . ."

"Who?"

"A neighbor of ours who was a good friend to the child. Verna Donovan. She's a divorcée; they were quite close."

I wrote the name down. "Go on."

"Anyway, Rheta said something about going for a walk with Mrs. Donovan. She also said she might go downtown and get some sheet music. I urged her to go out in the air, as it was a fine day, and gave her money for the music. After she left, I went for a walk myself, through the neighborhood. It was an unusually beautiful day for November, pleasantly warm."

"How long were you gone?"

"I returned at about four-forty-five. I came in the front door. Miss Shaunesey arrived from school about six o'clock. I wasn't worried then about Rheta's absence, because I expected her along at any minute. I prepared dinner for the three of us—Miss Shaunesey, Rheta and myself—and set the table. Finally, Miss Shaunesey and I sat down to eat . . . both wondering where Rheta was, but again, not terribly worried."

"It wasn't unusual for her to stay out without calling to say she'd miss supper?"

"Not in the least. She was quiet, but rather . . . self-absorbed. If she walked by a motion-picture marquee that caught her eye, she might just wander on in, without a thought about anyone who might be waiting for her."

"She sounds inconsiderate."

Alice Wynekoop smiled tightly, revealing a strained patience. "She was a strange, quiet girl. Rather moody, I'm afraid. She had definite feelings of inferiority, particularly in regards to my daughter, Catherine, who is after all a physician. But I digress. At about a quarter to seven, I telephoned Mrs. Donovan and asked her if she had been with Rheta. She said she hadn't seen her since three o'clock, but urged me not to worry."

"Were you worried?"

"Not terribly. At any rate, at about seven o'clock I asked Miss Shaunesey to go and get a prescription filled for me. She left the house and I remained there. She returned about an hour later and was surprised that Rheta had not yet returned. At this point, I admit I was getting worried about the girl."

"Tell me about finding the body."

She nodded, her eyes fixed. "Miss Shaunesey and I sat and talked in the library. Then about eight-thirty she asked me to get her some medicine for an upset stomach. I went downstairs to the examination room to get the medicine from the cabinet." She placed a finger against one cheek, thoughtfully. "I recall now that I thought it odd to find the door of the examination room closed, as it was usually kept open. I turned the knob and slipped my hand inside to find the electric switch."

"And you found her."

She shuddered, but it seemed a gesture, not an involuntary response. "It is impossible for me to describe my feelings when I saw Rheta lying there under that flood of light! I felt as if I were somewhere else. I cannot find words to express my feelings."

"What did you do?"

"Well, I knew something had to be done at once, and I called my daughter, Catherine, at the county hospital. I told her Rheta was dead. She was terribly shocked, of course. I . . . I thought I had asked Catherine to notify the coroner and to hurry right over. It seemed ages till she got there. When she did arrive, I had her call Dr. Berger and Mr. Ahearn. It wasn't until some time after they arrived that I realized Catherine had not called the coroner as I thought I'd instructed her. Mr. Ahearn then called the authorities."

I nodded. "All right. You're doing fine, Doctor. Now tell me about your son and his wife."

"What do you mean?"

"It wasn't a happy union, was it."

Her smile was a sad crease in her wrinkled face. "At one time it was. Earle went with me to a medical convention in Indianapolis in . . . must have been '29. Rheta played the violin as part of the entertainment, there. They began to correspond. A year later they were wed."

"And came to live with you."

"Earle didn't have a job—you know, he's taken up photography of late, and has had several assignments, I'm really very proud—and, well . . . anyway. The girl was barely nineteen when they married. I redecorated and refurnished a suite of rooms on the second floor for my newlyweds. She was a lovely child, beautiful red hair, and of course, Earle . . . he's as handsome a boy as ever walked this earth."

"But Rheta was moody . . . ?"

"Very much so. And obsessed with her health. Perhaps that's why she married into the Wynekoop family. She was fearful of tuberculosis, but there were no indications of it at all. In the last month of her life, she was rather melancholy, of a somewhat morbid disposition. I discussed with her about going out into the open and taking exercise. We discussed that often."

"You did not kill your daughter-in-law."

"No! Mr. Heller, I'm a doctor. My profession, my life, is devoted to healing."

I rose. Slipped the notebook in my pocket. "Well, thank you, Dr. Wynekoop. I may have a few more questions at a later date."

She smiled again, a warm, friendly smile, coming from so controlled a woman. "I'd be pleased to have your company. And I appreciate your help. I'm very worried about the effect this is having on Earle."

"Dr. Wynekoop, with all due respect . . . my major concern is the effect this going to have on you if I can't find the real killer."

Her smile disappeared and she nodded sagely. She extended her hand for a final handshake, and I left her there.

I used a pay phone in the visitors' area to call Sergeant Lou Sapperstein at Central Headquarters in the Loop. Lou had been my boss on the pickpocket detail. I asked him to check for me to see what officer in the Fillmore district had caught the call the night of the Wynekoop homicide.

"That's Stege's case," Lou said. Sapperstein was a hardnosed, fair-minded, balding cop of about forty-five seasoned years. "You shouldn't mess in Stege's business. He doesn't like you."

"God you're a great detective, picking up on a detail like that. Can you get me the name?"

"Five minutes. Stay where you are."

I gave him the pay phone number and he called back in a little over three minutes.

"Officer Raymond March, detailed with squad fifteen," he said.

I checked my watch; it was after four.

"He's on duty now," I said. "Do me another favor."

"Why don't you get a goddamn secretary?"

"You're a public servant, aren't you? So serve, already."

"So tell me what you want, already."

"Get somebody you trust at Fillmore to tell Officer March to meet me at the drugstore on the corner of Madison and Kedzie. Between six and seven."

"What's in it for Officer March?"

"Supper and a fin."

"Why not," Lou said, a shrug in his voice.

He called me back in five or six minutes and said the message would be passed.

I hit the streetcars again and was back on Monroe Street by a quarter to five. It was getting dark already, and colder.

Mrs. Verna Donovan lived in the second-floor two-flat of a graystone three doors down from the Wynekoop mansion. The smell of corned beef and cabbage cooking seeped from under the door.

I knocked.

It took a while, but a slender, attractive woman of perhaps thirty in a floral dress and a white apron opened the door wide.

"Oh!" she said. Her face was oblong, her eyes a luminous brown, her hair another agreeable shade of brown, cut in a bob that was perhaps too young for her.

"Didn't mean to startle you, ma'am. Are you Mrs. Donovan?"

"Yes." She smiled shyly. "Sorry for my reaction—I was expecting my son. We'll be eating in about half an hour . . ."

"I know this is a bad time to come calling. Perhaps I could arrange another time . . ."

"What is your business here?"

I gave her one of my A-1 Detective Agency cards. "I'm working for the Wynekoops. Nathan Heller, president of the A-1 agency. I'm hoping to find Rheta's killer."

Her eyes sparkled. "Well, come in! If you don't mind sitting in the kitchen while I get dinner ready . . ."

"Not at all," I said, following her through a nicely but not lavishly furnished living room, overseen by an elaborate print of the Virgin Mary, and back to a good-size, blue-and-white kitchen.

She stood at the counter making cole slaw while I sat at the kitchen table nearby.

"We were very good friends, Rheta and I. She was a lovely girl, talented, very funny."

"Funny? I get the impression she was a somber girl."

"Around the Wynekoops she was. They're about as much fun as falling down the stairs. Do you think the old girl killed her?"

"What do you think?"

"I could believe it of Earle. Dr. Alice herself, well . . . I mean, she's a doctor. She's aloof, and she and Rheta were anything but close, of course. But kill her?"

"I'm hearing that the doctor gave Rheta gifts, treated her like a family member."

Verna Donovan shrugged, putting some muscle into her slaw-making efforts. "There was no love lost between them. You're aware that Earle ran around on her?"

"Yes."

"Well, that sort of thing is hard on a girl's self-esteem. I helped her get over it as much as I could."

"How?"

She smiled slyly over her shoulder. "I'm a divorcée, Mr. Heller. And divorcées know how to have a good time. Care for a taste?"

She was offering me a forkful of slaw.

"That's nice," I said, savoring it. "Nice bite to it. So, you and Rheta went out together? Was she seeing other men, then?"

"Of course she was. Why shouldn't she?"

"Anyone in particular?"

"Her music teacher. Violin instructor. Older man, very charming. But he died of a heart attack four months ago. It hit her hard."

"How did she handle it?"

"Well, she didn't shoot herself in the back over it, if that's what you're thinking! She was morose for about a month . . . then she just started to date all of a sudden. I encouraged her, and she came back to life again."

"Why didn't she just divorce Earle?"

"Why, Mr. Heller . . . she was a good Catholic girl."

She asked me to stay for supper, but I declined, despite the tempting aroma of her corned beef and cabbage, and the tang of her slaw. I had another engagement, at a drugstore at Madison and Kedzie.

While I waited for Officer March to show up, I questioned the pharmacist behind the back counter.

"Sure I remember Miss Shaunesey stopping by that night," he said. "But I don't understand why she did."

"Why is that?"

"Well, Dr. Wynekoop herself stopped in a week before, to fill a similar prescription, and I told her our stock was low."

"She probably figured you'd've got some in by then," I said.

"The doctor knows we only get a shipment in once a month."

I was mulling that over at the lunch counter when Officer March arrived. He was in his late twenties and blond and much too fresh-faced for a Chicago cop.

"Nate Heller," he said, with a grin. "I've heard about you." We shook hands.

"Don't believe everything Captain Stege tells you," I said.

He took the stool next to me, took off his cap. "I know Stege thinks you're poison. But that's 'cause he's an old-timer. Me,

I'm glad you helped expose those two crooked bastards."

"Let's not get carried away, Officer March. What's the point of being a cop in this town if you can't take home a little graft now and then?"

"Sure," March said. "But those guys were killers. West Side bootleggers."

"I'm a West Side boy myself," I said.

"So I understand. So what's your interest in the Wynekoop case?"

"The family hired me to help clear the old gal. Do you think she did it?"

He made a clicking sound in his cheek. "Hard one to call. She seemed pretty shook up, at the scene."

"Shook up like a grieved family member, or a murderer?"

"I couldn't read it."

"Order yourself a sandwich and then tell me about it."

He did. The call had come in at nine-fifty-nine over the police radio, about five blocks away from where he and his partner were patrolling.

"The girl's body was lying on that table," March said. "She was resting on her left front side with her left arm under her, with the right forearm extending upward so that her hand was about on a level with her chin, with her head on a white pillow. Her face was almost out of sight, but I could see that her mouth and nose were resting on a wet, crumpled towel. She'd been bleeding from the mouth."

"She was covered up, I understand," I said.

"Yes. I drew the covers down carefully, and saw that she'd been shot through the left side of the back. Body was cold. Dead about six hours, I'd guess."

"But that's just a guess."

"Yeah. The coroner can't nail it all that exact. It can be a few hours either direction, you know."

"No signs of a struggle."

"None. That girl laid down on that table herself—maybe at gunpoint, but whatever the case, she did it herself. Her clothes were lying about the floor at the foot of the examination table, dropped, not thrown, just as though she'd undressed in a leisurely fashion."

"What about the acid burns on the girl's face?"

"She was apparently chloroformed before she was shot. You know, that confession Stege got out of Dr. Wynekoop, that's how she said she did it."

The counterman brought us coffee.

"I'll be frank, Officer," I said, sipping the steaming java. "I just came on this job. I haven't had a chance to go down to a newspaper morgue and read the text of that confession."

He shrugged. "Well, it's easily enough summed up. She said her daughter-in-law was always wanting physical examinations. That afternoon, she went downstairs with the doctor for an exam, and first off, stripped, to weigh herself. She had a sudden pain in her side and Dr. Wynekoop suggested a whiff of chloroform as an anesthetic. The doc said she massaged the girl's side for about fifteen minutes, and . . . ."

"I'm remembering this from the papers," I said, nodding. "She claimed the girl 'passed away' on the examining table, and she panicked. Figured her career would be ruined, if it came out she'd accidentally killed her own daughter-in-law with an overdose of chloroform."

"Right. And then she remembered the old revolver in the desk, and fired a shot into the girl and tried to make it look like a robbery."

The counterman came and refilled our coffee cups.

"So," I said, "what do you make of the confession?"

"I think it's bullshit any way you look at it. Hell, she was grilled for almost three days, Heller—you know how valid *that* kind of confession is."

I sipped my coffee. "She may have thought her son was guilty, and was covering up for him."

"Well, her confession was certainly a self-serving one. After all, if she was telling the truth—or even if her confession was made up outa whole cloth, but got taken at face value—it'd make her guilty of nothing more than involuntary manslaughter."

I nodded. "Shooting a corpse isn't a felony."

"But she *had* to know her son didn't do it."

"Why?"

March smirked. "He sent her a telegram; he was in Peoria, a hundred and ninety miles away."

"Telegram? When did she receive this telegram?"

"Late afternoon. Funny thing, though."

"Oh?"

"Initially, Dr. Wynekoop said she'd seen Earle last on November twelfth, when he left on a trip to the Grand Canyon to take some photographs. But Earle came back to Chicago on the nineteenth, two days before the murder."

I damn near spilled my coffee. *"What?"*

He nodded emphatically. "He and his mother met at a restaurant, miles from home. They were seen sitting in a back booth, having an intense, animated, but hushed, conversation."

"You said Earle was in Peoria when his wife was killed..."

"He was. He left Chicago, quietly, the next day—drove to Peoria. And from Peoria he went to Kansas City."

"Do his alibis hold up? Peoria isn't Mars; he could've established an alibi and made a round-trip..."

"I thought you were working for the family?"

"I am. But if I proved Earle did it, they'd spring his mother."

March laughed hollowly. "She'd be pissed off at you, partner."

"I know. But I already got their retainer. So. Tell me. What did you hold back from the papers?"

It was standard practice to keep back a few details in a murder case; it helped clear up confessions from crazy people.

"I shouldn't," he said.

I handed him a folded fin.

He slipped it in the breast pocket of his uniform blouse.

"Hope for you yet," I said.

"Two items of interest," March said softly. "There were three bullets fired from that gun."

"Three? But Rheta was shot only once . . ."

"Right."

"Were the other bullets found?"

"No. We took that examining room apart. Then we took the house apart. Nothing."

"What do you make of that?"

"I don't know. You'd have to ask Stege . . . if you got nerve enough."

"You said two things."

March swallowed slowly. "This may not even come out at the trial. It's not necessarily good for the prosecution."

"Spill."

"The coroner's physician picked up on something of interest, even before the autopsy."

"What?"

"Rheta had syphilis."

"Jesus. You're kidding!"

"A very bad dose."

I sat and pondered that.

"We asked Earle to submit to a physical," March said, "and he consented."

"And?"

"And he's in perfect health."

I took the El back to the Loop and got off at Van Buren and Plymouth, where I had an office on the second floor of the corner building. I lived there, since I kept an eye on the building in lieu of paying rent. Before I went up, I drank in the bar downstairs for half an hour or so, chatting with bartender Buddy Gold, who was a friend. I asked him if he was following the Wynekoop case in the papers.

"That old broad is innocent," the lumpy-faced ex-boxer said. "It's a crime what they're doin' to her."

"What are they doing to her?"

"I saw her picture in the paper, in that jailhouse hospital bed. Damn shame, nice woman like that, with her charities and all."

"What about the dead girl? Maybe she was 'nice.'"

"Yeah, but some dope fiend did it. Why don't they find him and put him in jail?"

I said that was a good idea and had another beer. Then I went up to my office and pulled down the Murphy bed and flopped. It had been a long, weird day. I'd earned my fifteen bucks.

The phone woke me. When I opened my eyes, it was morning but the light filtering in around the drawn shades was gray. It would be a cold one. I picked up the receiver on the fifth ring.

"A-1 Detective Agency," I said.

"Nathan Heller?" a gravelly male voice demanded.

I sat on the edge of the desk, rubbing my eyes. "Speaking."

"This is Captain John Stege."

I slid off the desk. "What can I do for you?"

"Steer clear of my case, you son of a bitch."

"What case is that, Captain?"

Stege was a white-haired fireplug with dark-rimmed glasses, a meek-looking individual who could scare the hell out of you when he felt like it. He felt like it.

"You stay out of the goddamn Wynekoop case. I won't have you mucking it up."

How did he even know I was on the case? Had Officer March told him?

"I was hired by the family to try to help clear Dr. Wynekoop. It's hardly uncommon for a defendant in a murder case to hire an investigator."

"Dr. Alice Lindsay Wynekoop murdered her daughter-in-law! It couldn't be any other way."

"Captain, it could be a lot of other ways. It could be one of her boyfriends; it could be one of her husband's girlfriends. It could be a break-in artist looking for drugs. It could be . . ."

"Are you telling me how to do my job?"

"Well, you're telling me how not to do mine."

There was a long pause.

Then Stege said: "I don't like you, Heller. You stay out of my way. You go manufacturing evidence, and I'll introduce you to every rubber hose in town—and I know plenty of 'em."

"You have the wrong idea about me, Captain," I said. "And you may have the wrong idea about Alice Wynekoop."

"Bull! She insured young Rheta for five grand, fewer than thirty days before the girl's death. With double indemnity, the policy pays ten thousand smackers."

I hadn't heard about this.

"The Wynekoops *have* money," I said. "A murder-for-insurance-money scheme makes no sense for a well-to-do family like that . . ."

"Dr. Wynekoop owes almost five thousand dollars in back taxes and has over twenty thousand dollars in overdue bank notes. She's prominent, but she's not wealthy. She got hit in the crash."

"Well . . ."

"She killed her daughter-in-law to make her son happy and to collect the insurance money. If you were worth two cents as a detective, you'd know that."

"Speaking of detective work, Captain, how did you know I was on this case?"

"Don't you read the papers?"

The papers had me in them, all right. A small story, but well placed, on several front pages in fact; under a picture of Earle seated at his mother's side in the jail hospital, the *News* told how the Wynekoops had hired a local private investigator, one Nathan Heller, to help prove Dr. Alice's innocence.

I called Earle Wynekoop and asked him to meet me at the County Jail hospital wing. I wanted to talk to both of my clients.

On the El, I thought about how I had intended to pursue this case. Having done the basic groundwork with the family and witnesses, I would begin searching for the faceless break-in artist whose burglary had got out of hand, leading to the death of Rheta Wynekoop. Never mind that it made no sense for a thief to take a gun from a rolltop desk, make his victim undress, shoot her in the back, tuck her in like a child at bedtime, and leave the gun behind. Criminals did crazy things, after all. I would spend three or four days sniffing around the West Side pawn shops and resale shops, and the Maxwell Street market, looking for a lead on any petty crook whose drug addiction might lead to violence. I would comb the flophouses and bars hopheads were known to frequent, and . . .

But I had changed my mind, at least for the moment.

Earle was at his mother's bedside when the matron left me there. Dr. Alice smiled in her tight, businesslike manner and offered me a hand to shake; I took it. Earle stood and nodded and smiled nervously at me. I nodded to him, and he sat again.

But I stayed on my feet.

"I'm off this case," I said.

"What?" Earle said, eyes wide.

Dr. Alice remained calm. Her appraising eyes were as cold as the weather.

"Captain Stege suggested it," I said.

"That isn't legal!" Earle said.

"Quiet, Earle," his mother said, sternly but with gentleness.

"That's not why I'm quitting," I said. "And I'm keeping the retainer, too, by the way."

"Now that *isn't* legal!" Earle said, standing.

"Shut up," I said to him. To her, I said: "You two used me. I'm strictly a publicity gimmick. To help make you look sincere, to help you keep up a good front . . . just like staying in the jail's hospital ward, so you can pose for pitiful newspaper pics."

Dr. Alice blinked and smiled thinly. "You're revealing an obnoxious side, Mr. Heller, that is unbecoming."

"You killed your daughter-in-law, Dr. Wynekoop. For sonny boy, here."

Earle's face clenched like a fist, and he clenched his fists, too, while he was at it. "I ought to . . ."

I looked at him hard. "I wish to hell you would."

His eyes flickered at me, then he glanced at his mother. She nodded and motioned for him to sit again, and he did.

"Mr. Heller," she said, "I assure you, I am innocent. I don't know what you've been told that gave you this very false impression, but . . ."

"Save it. I know what happened, and why. You discovered, in one of your frequent on-the-house examinations of your hypochondriac daughter-in-law, that she really *was* ill. Specifically, she had a social disease."

Anger flared in the doctor's eyes.

"You could forgive Earle all his philandering . . . even though you didn't approve. You did ask your daughter to talk to him about his excesses of drink and dames. But those were just misdemeanors. For your wife to run around, to get a nasty disease that she might just pass along to your beloved boy, should their marriage ever heat up again, well, that was a crime. And it deserved punishment."

"Mr. Heller, why don't you go? You may keep your retainer, if you keep your silence."

"Oh, hitting a little close to home, am I? Well, let me finish. You paid for this. I don't think it was your idea to kill Rheta, despite the dose of syph she was carrying. I think it was Earle's idea. She wouldn't give him a divorce, good Catholic girl that she was, and Earle's a good Catholic, too, after all. It'd be hell to get excommunicated, right, Earle? Right, Mom?"

Earle was shaking; his hands clasped, prayerfully. Dr. Wynekoop's wrinkled face was a stern mask.

"Here's what happened," I said, cheerfully. "Earle came to you and asked you to put the little woman to sleep . . . she was a tortured girl, after all, if it were done painlessly, why, it would be a merciful act. But you refused—you're a doctor, a healer. It wouldn't be right."

Earle's eyes were shifting from side to side in confirmation of my theory.

I forged ahead: "But Earle came to you again, and said, Mother dear, if you don't do it, I will. I've found father's old .32, and I've tried it . . . fired two test rounds. It works, and I know how to work it. I'm going to kill Rheta myself."

Earle's eyes were wide as was his mouth. I must have come very, very close, even perhaps to his very language. Dr. Alice continued to maintain a poker face.

"So, Mom, you decided to take matters in hand. When Earle came back early from his Grand Canyon photo trip, the two of you rendezvoused away from home—though you were seen, unfortunately—and came up with a plan. Earle would resume his trip, only go no farther than Peoria, where he would establish an alibi."

Earle's face was contorted as he took in every damning word.

"On the day of the murder," I told her, "you had a final private consultation with your daughter-in-law . . . you over-dosed her with chloroform, or smothered her."

"Mr. Heller," Dr. Alice said icily, looking away from me, "this fantasy of yours holds no interest whatsoever for me."

"Well, maybe so—but Earle's all perked up. Anyway, you left the body downstairs, closing the examining room door, locking it probably, and went on about the business of business as usual . . . cooking supper for your roomer, spending a quiet evening with her . . . knowing that Earle would be back after dark, to quietly slip in and, what? Dispose of the body somehow. That was the plan, right? The unhappy bride would just disappear. Or perhaps turn up dead in ditch, or . . . whatever. Only it didn't happen that way. Because sonny boy chickened out."

And now Dr. Alice broke form, momentarily, her eyes turning on Earle for just a moment, giving him one nasty glance, the only time I ever saw her look at the louse with anything but devotion.

"He sent you a telegram in the afternoon, letting you know that he was still in Peoria. And that he was going to stay in Peoria. And you, with a corpse in the basement. Imagine."

"You have a strange sense of humor, Mr. Heller."

"You have a strange way of practicing medicine, Dr. Wynekoop. You sent your roomer, Miss Shaunesey, on a fool's errand—sending her to a drugstore where you knew the prescription couldn't be filled. And you knew conscientious Miss Shaunesey would try another drugstore, buying you time."

"Really," Dr. Alice said, dryly.

"Really. That's when you concocted the burglary story. You're too frail, physically, to go hauling a corpse anywhere. But you remembered that gun across the hall. So you shot your dead daughter-in-law, adding insult to injury, and faked the robbery—badly, but it was impromptu, after all."

"I don't have to listen to this!" Earle said.

"Then don't," I said. "What you didn't remember, Dr. Wynekoop, is that two bullets had already been fired from that weapon, when Earle tested it. And that little anomaly bothered me."

"Did it," she said, flatly.

"It did. Your daughter-in-law's syphilis; the two missing bullets; and the hour you spent alone in the house, while the roomer was away and Rheta was dead in your examining room. Those three factors added up to two things: your guilt and your son's complicity."

"Are you going to tell your story to anyone?" she asked, blandly.

"No," I said. "You're my client."

"How much?" Earle said, with a nasty, nervous little sneer.

I held my hands up, palms out. "No more. I'm keeping my retainer. I earned it."

I turned my back on them and began to walk away.

From behind me, I heard her say, with no irony whatsoever, "Thank you, Mr. Heller."

I turned and looked at her and laughed. "Hey, you're going to jail, lady. The cops and the D.A. won't need me to get it done, and all the good publicity you cook up won't change a thing. I have only one regret."

I made them ask.

Earle took the honors.

"What's that?" Earle asked, as he stood there trembling; his mother reached her hand out and patted his nearest hand, soothing him.

I smiled at him—the nastiest smile I could muster. "That you won't be going to jail with her, you son of a bitch."

*   *   *

And go to jail she did.

But it took a while. A most frail-looking Dr. Alice was carried into the courtroom on the opening day of the trial; still playing for sympathy in the press, I figured.

Then, after eight days of evidence, Dr. Alice had an apparent heart seizure when the prosecution hauled the blood-stained examination table into court. A mistrial was declared. When she recovered, though, she got a brand-new one. The press milked the case for all its worth; public opinion polls in the papers indicated half of Chicago considered Dr. Alice guilty, and the other half thought her innocent. The jury, however, was unanimous—it took them only fifteen minutes to find her guilty and two hours to set the sentence at twenty-five years.

Earle didn't attend the trial. They say that just as Dr. Alice was being ushered in the front gate at the Woman's Reformatory at Dwight, Illinois, an unshaven, disheveled figure darted from the nearby bushes. Earle kissed his mother goodbye and she brushed away his tears. As usual.

She served thirteen years, denying her guilt all the way; she was released with time off for good behavior. She died on July 4, 1955, in a nursing home, under an assumed name.

Earle changed his name, too. What became of him, I can't say. There were rumors, of course. One was that he had found work as a garage mechanic.

Another was that he had finally re-married—a beautiful redhead.

Dr. Catherine Wynekoop did not change her name and went on to a distinguished medical career.

And the house at 3406 West Monroe, the Death Clinic, was torn down in 1947. The year Dr. Alice was released.

HOUSE CALL

N INETEEN-THIRTY-SIX BEGAN FOR ME WITH a missing persons case. It didn't stay a missing persons case long, but on that bitterly cold Chicago morning of January third, all Mrs. Peacock knew was that her doctor husband had failed to come home after making a house call the night before.

It was Saturday, just a little past ten, and I was filling out an insurance adjustment form when she knocked. I said come in, and she did, an attractive woman of about thirty-five in an expensive fur coat. She didn't look high-hat, though: she'd gone out today without any make-up on, which, added to her generally haggard look, told me she was at wit's end.

"Mr. Heller? Nathan Heller?"

I said I was, standing, gesturing to a chair across from my desk. My office at the time was a large single room on the fourth floor of a less than fashionable building on the corner of Van Buren and Plymouth, in the shadow of the El. She seemed a little posh to be coming to my little one-man agency for help.

"Your name was given to me by Tom Courtney," she said.

"He's a friend of the family."

State's Attorney Thomas J. Courtney and I had crossed paths several times, without any particular mishap; this explained why she'd chosen the A-1 Detective Agency but not why she needed a detective in the first place.

"My husband is missing," she said.

"I assume you've filed a missing person's report."

"Yes I have. But I've been told until twenty-four hours elapse, my husband will not be considered missing. Tom suggested if my concern was such that I felt immediate action warranted, I might contact you. Which I have."

She was doing an admirable job of maintaining her composure; but there was a quaver in her voice and her eyes were moist.

"If you have any reason to suspect a kidnapping or foul play," I said, keeping my voice calm and soft to lessen the impact of such menacing words, "I think you're doing the right thing. Trails can go cold in twenty-four hours."

She nodded, found a brave smile.

"My husband, Silber, is a doctor, a pediatrician. We live in the Edgewater Beach Apartments."

That meant money; no wonder she hadn't questioned me about my rates.

"Last evening Betty Lou, our eight-year-old, and I returned home from visiting my parents in Bowen. Silber met us at Union Station and we dined at little restaurant on the North Side—the name escapes me, but I could probably come up with it if it proves vital—and then came home. Silber went to bed; I was sitting up reading. The phone rang. The voice was male. I asked for a name, an address, the nature of the business, doing my best to screen the call. But the caller insisted on talking to the doctor. I was reluctant, but I called Silber to the phone, and I heard him say, 'What is it? . . . . Oh, a child is ill?

Give me the address and I'll be there straight away.'"

"Did your husband write the address down?"

She nodded. "Yes, and I have the sheet right here." She dug in her purse and handed it to me.

In the standard, barely readable prescription-pad scrawl of any doctor, the note said: "G. Smale. 6438 North Whipple Street."

"Didn't the police want this?"

She shook her head no. "Not until it's officially a missing persons case they don't."

"No phone number?"

"My husband asked for one and was told that the caller had no phone."

"Presumably he was calling on one."

She shrugged, with sad frustration. "I didn't hear the other end of the conversation. All I can say for certain is that my husband hung up, sighed, smiled and said, 'No rest for the wicked,' and dressed. I jotted the information from the pad onto the top of the little Chicago street guide he carries when he's doing house calls."

"So he never took the original note with him?"

"No. What you have there is what he wrote. Then Silber kissed me, picked up his black instrument bag and left. I remember glancing at the clock in the hall. It was ten-oh-five p.m."

"Did you hear from him after that?"

"No I did not. I slept, but fitfully, and woke around one-thirty a.m. Silber wasn't home yet. I remember being irritated with him for taking a call from someone who wasn't a regular patient; he has an excellent practice, now—there's no need for it. I called the building manager and asked if Silber's car had returned to the garage. It hadn't. I didn't sleep a wink after that. When dawn broke, so, I'm afraid, did I. I called Tom Courtney;

he came around at once, phoned the police for me, then advised me to see you, should I feel the need for immediate action."

"I'm going to need some further information," I said.

"Certainly."

Questioning her, I came up with a working description and other pertinent data: Peacock was forty years old, a member of the staff of Children's Memorial. He'd been driving a 1931 black Cadillac sedan, 1936 license 25-682. Wearing a gray suit, gray topcoat, gray felt hat. 5' 7", 150 lbs., wire-frame glasses.

I walked her down to the street and helped her hail a cab. I told her I'd get right on the case, and that in the future she needn't call on me; I'd come to her at her Edgewater Beach apartment. She smiled, rather bravely I thought, as she slipped into the backseat of the cab, squeezed my arm and looked at me like I was something noble.

Well, I didn't feel very noble. Because as her cab turned down Plymouth Court, I was thinking that her husband the good doctor had probably simply had himself a big evening. He'd show up when his head stopped throbbing, or when something below the belt stopped throbbing, anyway. In the future he'd need to warn his babe to stop calling him at home, even if she did have a brother or a knack for doing a convincing vocal imitation of a male.

Back in my office I got out the private detective's most valuable weapon—the telephone book—and looked up G.W. Smale. There was a listing with the same street number— 6438—but the street was wrong, South Washtenaw. The names and house numbers tallied, yes, but the streets in question were on opposite sides of the city. The reverse directory listing street numbers followed by names and numbers told me that no "G. Smale" was listed at 6438 North Whipple.

What the hell; I called the Smale on South Washtenaw.

"I don't know any Dr. Peacock," he said. "I never saw the man in my life."

"Who do you take your kids to when they're sick?"

"Nobody."

"Nobody?"

"I don't have any kids. I'm not a father."

I talked to him for fifteen minutes, and he seemed forthright enough; my instincts, and I do a lot of phone work, told me to leave him to the cops, or at least till later that afternoon. I wanted to check out the doctor's working quarters.

So I tooled my sporty '32 Auburn over to 4753 Broadway, where Dr. Peacock shared sumptuous digs with three other doctors, highly reputable medical specialists all. His secretary was a stunning brunette in her late twenties, a Miss Kathryn Mulrooney. I like a good-looking woman in white; the illusion of virginity does something for me.

"I know what you're going to ask," she said, quickly, before I'd asked anything. All I'd done was show her my investigator's I.D. and say I was in Mrs. Peacock's employ. "Dr. Peacock had no patient named Smale; I've been digging through our files ever since Mrs. Peacock called this morning, just in case my memory is faulty."

She didn't look like she had a faulty anything.

"What's even stranger," she said, with a tragic expression, "he almost never answered night calls. Oh, he once upon a time did—he hated to turn away any sick child. His regular patients seldom asked him to do so, however, and this practice has become so large that he wasn't accepting any new cases. It's unbelievable that . . ."

She paused; I'd been doing my job, asking questions, listening, but a certain part of me had been undressing the attractive woman in my mind's eye—everybody needs a hobby—and she misread my good-natured lechery toward her for something else.

"Please!" she said. "You mustn't leap to horrid conclusions. Dr. Peacock was a man of *impeccable* character. He loved his family and his home, passionately. He was no playboy; he loathed nightclubs and all they stand for. He didn't even drink!"

"I see," I said.

"I hope you do," she said curtly. "That he might have been involved in an affair with a woman other than his wife is unthinkable. Please believe me."

"Perhaps I do. But could you answer one question?"

"What's that?"

"Why are you referring to the doctor in the past tense?"

She began to cry; she'd been standing behind a counter— now she leaned against it.

"I . . . I wish I believed him capable of running around on Ruth, his wife. Then I wouldn't be so convinced that something . . . something *terrible* has happened."

I felt bad; I'd been suspicious of her, been looking to find her between the doctor's sheets, and had made her cry. She was a sincere young woman, that was obvious.

"I'm very sorry," I said, meaning it, and turned to go.

But before I went out, another question occurred to me, and I asked it: "Miss Mulrooney—had the parents of any patient ever blamed Dr. Peacock for some unfortunate results of some medical treatment he administered? Any threats of reprisal?"

"Absolutely not," she said, chin trembling.

On this point I didn't believe her; her indignation rang shrill. And, anyway, most doctors make enemies. I only wished she had pointed to one of those enemies.

But I'd pushed this kid enough.

I dropped by the Edgewater Beach Apartments—not to talk

to Mrs. Peacock. I went up to the attendant in the lobby, a distinguished-looking blue-uniformed man in his late fifties; like so many doormen and lobby attendants, he looked like a soldier from some foreign country in a light opera.

Unlike a good solider, he was willing to give forth with much more than his name and rank. I had hoped to get from him the name of the night man, who I hoped to call and get some information from; but it turned out *he* was the night man.

"George was sick," he said. "So I'm doing double-duty. I can use the extra cash more than the sleep."

"Speaking of cash," I said, and handed him a buck.

"Thank you, sir!"

"Now, earn it: what can you tell me about Dr. Peacock? Does he duck out at night very often?"

The attendant shook his head no. "Can't remember the last time, before the other night. Funny thing, though."

"Yeah?"

"He was rushing out of here, then all of a sudden stopped and turned and stood five minutes blabbing in the phone booth over there."

Back in the Auburn, my mind was abuzz. Why else would Dr. Peacock use the lobby phone, unless it was to make a call he didn't want his wife to hear? The "poor sick child" call had been a ruse. The baby specialist obviously had a babe.

I didn't have a missing persons case at all. I had a stray husband who had either taken off for parts unknown with his lady love or, more likely considering the high-hat practice the doc would have to leave behind, would simply show up with some cock-and-bull story for the missus after a torrid twenty-four-hour shack-up with whoever-she-was.

I drove to 6438 North Whipple Street. What my reverse phone book hadn't told me was that this was an apartment building, a six-flat. Suddenly the case warmed up again; I found a place for the Auburn along the curb and walked up the steps into the brownstone.

No "G. Smale" was a resident, at least not a resident who had a name on any of the vestibule mailboxes.

I walked out into the cold air, my breath smoking, my mind smoking a little too: the "patient" hadn't had a phone, but in a nice brownstone like this most likely *everybody* had a phone. Nothing added up. Except maybe two plus two equals rendez-vous.

The doc had a doll, that's all there was to it. Nonetheless, I decided to scout the neighborhood for Peacock's auto. I went two blocks in all directions and saw no sign of it. I was about to call it an afternoon, and a long one at that, when I extended the canvassing to include a third block, and on the 6000 block in North Francisco Avenue, I saw it: a black Caddy sedan with the license 25-682.

I approached the car, which was parked alongside a vacant lot, across from several brownstones. I peeked in; in the backseat was a topcoat, but the topcoat was covering something. Looking in the window, you couldn't tell what. I tried the door. It was unlocked.

I pulled the rider's seat forward, and there he was, in a kneeling position, in the back, facing the rear, the top half of him bent over the seat, covered by the topcoat. Carefully, I lifted it off, resting it on the hood of the car. Blood was spattered on the floor and rear windows; the seat was crusty black with it, dried. His blood-flecked felt hat, wadded up like a discarded tissue, lay on the seat. His medical bag was on the seat next to him; it too had been sheltered from sight by the topcoat, and was open and had been disturbed. The little street map book, with the address on it in Mrs. Peacock's handwriting, was nearby, speckled with blood.

A large caliber bullet had gone in his right temple and come out behind the left ear. His skull was crushed; his brain was showing, but scrambled. His head and shoulders bore numerous knife slashes. His right hand was gloved, but his left was bare and had been caught, crushed, in the slamming car door.

This was one savage killing.

Captain Stege himself arrived, after I called it in; if my name hadn't been attached to it, he probably wouldn't have come. The tough little cop had once been Chief of Detectives till, ironically, a scandal had cost him—one of Chicago's few verifiably honest cops—his job. Not long ago he'd been chief of the PD's Dillinger squad. It was on the Dillinger case that Stege and I had put our feud behind us; we were uneasily trying to get along these days.

I quickly showed him two more discoveries I'd made before he or any of his boys in blue had arrived: a .45 revolver shell that was in the snow, near the car, on the vacant lot side; and a pinkish stain in the snow, plus deep tire tracks and numerous cigarette butts, in front of the apartment building at 6438 North Whipple. The tire tracks and cigarettes seemed to indicate that whoever had lured the doctor from his bed had indeed waited at this address; the pink stain pointed toward the violence having started there.

"What's your part in this?" he said, as we walked back to the scene of the crime. He was a small gray man in a gray topcoat and gray formless hat; tiny eyes squinted behind round, black-rimmed lenses. "How'd you happen to find the body, anyway?"

I explained that Mrs. Peacock had hired me to find her husband. Which, after all, I had.

A police photographer was taking pictures, the body not yet moved.

"How do you read this, Heller?"

"Not a simple robbery."

"Oh?"

I pointed to the corpse. "He took God knows how many brutal blows; he was slashed and slashed again. It takes hate to arouse pointless violence like that."

"Crime of passion, then."

"That's how I see it, Captain."

"The wife have an alibi?"

"Don't even bother going down that road."

"You mind if I bother, Heller? You ever seen the statistics of the number of murders committed within families?"

"She was home with her daughter. Go ahead. Waste your time. But she's a nice lady."

"I'll remember that. Give your statement to Phelan, and go home. This isn't your case, anymore."

"I know it isn't. But do you mind if I, uh . . . if I'm the one to break the news to Mrs. Peacock?"

Stege cleared his throat; shot a wad of phlegm into the nearby snow. "Not at all. Nobody envies duty like that."

So I told her. I wanted her told by somebody who didn't suspect her and, initially, I'd be the only one who qualified.

She sat in a straightback chair at her dining room table, in the Peacocks' conservative yet expensively appointed apartment high in the Edgewater Beach, and wept into a lace hanky. I sat with her for fifteen minutes. She didn't ask me to go, so I didn't.

Finally she said, "Silber was a fine man. He truly was. A perfect husband and father. His habits regular and beyond reproach. No one hated Silber. No one. He was lured to his death by thieves."

"Yes, ma'am."

"Did you know that once before he was attacked by thieves, and that he did not hesitate to fight them off? My husband was a brave man."

"I'm sure he was."

I left her there, with her sorrow, thinking that I wished she was right, but knowing she was wrong. I did enough divorce work to know how marriages, even "perfect" ones, can go awry. I also had a good fix on just how much marital cheating was going on in this Christian society.

The next morning I called Stege. He wasn't glad to hear from me, exactly, but he did admit that the wife was no longer a suspect; her alibi was flawless.

"There *was* a robbery of sorts," Stege said.

"Oh?"

"Twenty dollars was missing from Peacock's wallet. On the other hand, none of his jewelry—some of it pretty expensive stuff—was even touched."

"What was taken from the medical bag?" I asked.

"Some pills and such were taken, but apparently nothing narcotic. A baby specialist doesn't go toting dope around."

"An addict might not know that; an addict might've picked Dr. Peacock's name at random, not knowing he was a baby doc."

"And, what? Drew him to that vacant lot to steal a supposed supply of narcotics?"

"Yeah. It might explain the insanity, the savagery of the attack."

"Come on, Heller. You know as well as I do this is a personal killing. I expect romance to rear its lovely head any time, now. Peacock was rich, handsome enough, by all accounts personable. And he had, we estimate, upwards of five hundred patients. Five hundred kiddies all of whom have mothers who visited the doctor with them."

"You know something, Captain?"

"What?"

"I'm glad this isn't my case anymore."

"Oh?"

"Yeah. I wish you and your boys all the best doing those five hundred interviews."

He grumbled and hung up.

I did send Mrs. Peacock a bill, for one day's services—twenty dollar and five dollars for expenses—and settled back to watch, with some discomfort, the papers speculate about the late doctor's love life. Various screwball aspects to the case were chased down by the cops and the press; none of it amounted to much. This included a nutty rumor that the doctor was a secret federal narcotics agent and killed by a dope ring; and the Keystone Kops affair of the mysterious key found in the doctor's pocket, the lock to which countless police hours were spent seeking, only to have the key turn out to belong to the same deputy coroner who had produced it. The hapless coroner had accidentally mixed a key of his own among the Peacock evidence.

More standard, reliable lines of inquiry provided nothing: fingerprints found in the car were too smudged to identify; witnesses who came forth regarding two people arguing in the death car varied as to the sex of the occupants; the last-minute phone call Peacock made in the lobby turned out to have been to one of his business partners; interviews of the parents of five hundred Peacock patients brought forth not a single disgruntled person, nor a likely partner for any Peacock "love nest."

Peacock had been dead for over two weeks, when I was brought back into the case again, through no effort of my own.

The afternoon of January sixteenth, someone knocked at my office door; in the middle of a phone credit check, I covered the receiver and called out, "Come in."

The door opened tentatively and a small, Milquetoast of a man peered in.

"Mr. Heller?"

I nodded, motioned for him to be seated before me, and finished up my call; he sat patiently, a pale little man in a dark suit, his dark hat in his lap.

"What can I do for you?"

He stood, smiled in an entirely humorless, businesslike manner, extending a hand to be shook; I shook it, and the grip was surprisingly firm.

"I am a Lutheran minister," he said. "My name, for the moment, is unimportant."

"Pleased to meet you, Reverend."

"I read about the Peacock case in the papers."

"Yes?"

"I saw your name. You discovered the body. You were in Mrs. Peacock's employ."

"Yes."

"I have information. I was unsure of whom to give it to."

"If you have information regarding the Peacock case, you should give it to the police. I can place a call right now . . ."

"Please, no! I would prefer you hear my story and judge for yourself."

"All right."

"Last New Year's Day I had a chance meeting with my great and good friend, Dr. Silber Peacock, God rest his soul. On that occasion the doctor confided that a strange man, a fellow who claimed to be a chiropodist, had come bursting into his office, making vile accusations."

"Such as?"

"He said, 'You, sir, are having an affair with my wife!'"

I sat forward. "Go on."

"Dr. Peacock said he'd never laid eyes on this man before; that he thought him a crazy man. 'Why, I never ran around on Ruth in my life,' he said."

"How did he deal with this man?"

"He threw him bodily from his office."

"When did he have this run-in? Did he mention the man's name?"

"Last October. The man's name was Thompson, and he was, as I've said, a chiropodist."

"You should go to the police with this."

The Reverend stood quickly, nervously. "I'd really rather not."

And then he was on his way out of the office. By the time I got out from behind my desk, he was out of the room, and by the time I got out into the hall, he was out of sight.

The only chiropodist named Thompson in the Chicago phone book was one Arthur St. George Thompson, whom I found at his Wilson Avenue address. He was a skinny, graying man in his early forties; he and his office were seedy. He had no patients in his rather unkempt waiting room when I arrived (or when I left, for that matter).

"I knew Silber Peacock," he said, bitterly. "I remember visiting him at his office in October, too. What of it?"

"Did you accuse him of seeing your wife?"

"Sure I did! Let me tell you how I got hep to Peacock and Arlene. One evening last June she came home stinking, her and Ann—that's the no-good who's married to Arlene's brother Carl. Arlene said she'd been at the Subway Club and her escort was Doc Peacock. So I looked in the classified directory. The only Dr. Peacock was Silber C., so I knew it was him. I stewed about it for weeks, months, and then I went to his office. The son of a bitch pretended he didn't know who I was, or Arlene, either; he just kept denying it, and shoving me out of there, shoved me clear out into the hall."

"I see."

"No you don't. I hated the louse, but I didn't kill him.

Besides, I got an alibi. I can prove where I was the night he was murdered."

He claimed that because his practice was so poor of late, he'd taken on menial work at the Medinah Club. An alibi out of a reputable place like that would be hard to break. I'd leave that to Stege, when—or if—I turned this lead over to him.

First I wanted to talk to Arlene Thompson, who I found at her brother's place, a North Side apartment.

Ann was a slender, giggly brunette, attractive. Arlene was even more attractive, a voluptuous redhead. Both were in their mid-twenties. Ann's husband wasn't home, so the two of them flirted with me and we had a gay old time.

"Were you really seeing Doc Peacock?"

The two girls exchanged glances and began giggling and the giggling turned to outright laughter. "That poor guy!" Arlene said.

"Well, yeah, I'd say so. He's dead."

"Not him! Arthur! That insane streak of jealousy's got him in hot water again, has it? Look, good-lookin'—there's nothing *to* any of this, understand? Here's how it happened."

Arlene and Ann had gone alone to the Subway Cafe one afternoon, a rowdy honky-tonk that had since lost its liquor license, and got picked up by two men. They danced till dusk. Arlene's man said he was Doc Peacock; no other first name given.

"Arthur went off his rocker when I came in, tipsy. He demanded the truth—so I told it to him! It was all innocent enough, but it got him goin'. He talked days on end about Doc Peacock, about how he was going to even the score."

"Do you think he did?"

The redhead laughed again, said, "Honey, that Dr. Peacock whose puss has been in the papers ain't the guy I dated. My Peacock was much better looking—wavy hair, tall, a real dreamboat. I think my pick-up just pulled a name out of his hat."

"Your husband didn't know that. Maybe he evened the score with the wrong Peacock."

She shook her head, not believing that for a minute. "Arthur just isn't the type. He's a poor, weak sister. He never had enough pep to hurt a fly."

It was all conjecture, but I turned it over to Stege, anyway. Thompson's alibi checked out. Yet another dead-end.

The next day I was reading the morning papers over breakfast in the coffee shop at the Morrison Hotel. A very small item, buried on an inside page, caught my eye: Dr. Joseph Soldinger, 1016 North Oakley Blvd., had been robbed at gunpoint last night of thirty-seven dollars, his car stolen.

I called Stege and pointed out the similarity to the Peacock case, half expecting him to shrug it off. He didn't. He thanked me and hung up.

A week later I got a call from Stege; he was excited. "Listen to this: Dr. A.L. Abrams, 1600 Milwaukee Avenue, fifty-six dollars lost to gunmen; Dr. L.A. Garness, 2542 Mozart Avenue, waylaid and robbed of six dollars. And there's two more like that."

"Details?"

"Each features a call to a doctor to rush to a bedside. Address is in a lonely neighborhood. It's an appointment with ambush. Take is always rather small. Occurrences between ten and eleven p.m."

"Damn! Sounds like Mrs. Peacock has been right all along. Her husband fought off his attackers; that's what prompted their beating him."

"The poor bastard was a hero and the papers paint him a philanderer."

"Well, we handed 'em the brush."

"Perhaps we did, Heller. Anyway, thanks."

"Any suspects?"

"No. But we got the pattern now. From eyewitness descriptions it seems to be kids. Four assailants, three tall and husky, the other shorter."

A bell was ringing, and not outside my window. "Captain, you ever hear of Rose Kasallis?"

"Can't say I have."

"I tracked a runaway girl to her place two summers ago. She's a regular female Fagin. She had a flat on North Maplewood Avenue that was a virtual 'school for crime.'"

"I have heard of that. The West North Avenue cops handled it. She was keeping a waystation for fugitive kids from the reform school at St. Charles. Sent up the river for contributing to the delinquency of minors?"

"That's the one. I had quite a run-in with her charming boy Bobby. Robert Goethe is his name."

"Oh?"

"He's eighteen years old, a strapping kid with the morals of an alley cat. And there were a couple of kids he ran with, Emil Reck, who they called Emil the Terrible, and another one whose name I can't remember . . ."

"Heller, Chicago has plenty of young street toughs. Why do you think these three might be suspects in the Peacock case?"

"I don't know that they are. In fact, last I knew Bobby and the other two were convicted of strong-arming a pedestrian and were sitting in the Bridewell. But that's been at least a year ago."

"And they might be out amongst us again, by now."

"Right. Could you check?"

"I'll do that very thing."

Ten minutes later Stege called and said, "They were released in December."

January second had been Silber Peacock's last day on earth.
"I have an address for Bobby Goethe's apartment," Stege
said. "Care to keep an old copper company?"

He swung by and picked me up—hardly usual procedure,
pulling in a private dick on a case, but I had earned this—and
soon we were pulling up in front of the weathered brownstone
in which Bobby Goethe lived. And there was no doubt he lived
here.

Because despite the chilly day, he and Emil the Terrible
were sitting on the stoop, in light jackets, smoking cigarettes
and drinking bottles of beer. Bobby had a weak, acned chin,
and reminded me of photos I'd seen of Clyde Barrow; Emil
had a big lumpy nose and a high forehead, atop which was
piled blond curly hair—he looked thick as a plank.

We were in an unmarked car, but a uniformed man was
behind the wheel, so as soon as we pulled in, the two boys
reacted, beer bottles dropping to the cement and exploding like
bombs.

Bobby took off in one direction, and Emil took off in the
other. Stege just watched as his plainclothes detective assistant took off after Emil, and I took off after Bobby.

It took me a block to catch up, and I hit him with a flying
tackle, and we rolled into a vacant lot, not unlike the one by the
Caddy in which Peacock's body had been found.

Bobby was a wiry kid, and wormed his way out of my grasp,
kicking back at me as he did; I took a boot in the face, but didn't
lose any teeth, and managed to reach out and grab that foot and
yank him back hard. He went down on his face in the weeds
and rocks. One of the larger of those rocks found its way into
his hand, and he flung it at me, savage little animal that he was,
only not so little. I ducked out of the rock's way, but quickly
reached a hand under my topcoat and suitcoat and got my nine
millimeter Browning out and pointed it down at him.

"I'm hurt," he said, looking up at me with a scraped, bloody face.

"Shall we call a doctor?" I said.

Emil and Bobby and their crony named Nash, who was arrested later that afternoon by West North Avenue Station cops, were put in a show-up for the various doctors who'd been robbed to identify. They did so, without hesitation. The trio was separated and questioned individually and sang and sang. A fourth boy was implicated, the shorter one who'd been mentioned, seventeen-year-old Mickey Livingston. He too was identified, and he too sang.

Their story was a singularly stupid one. They had been cruising in a stolen car, stopped in a candy store, picked Peacock's name at random from the phone book, picked another name and address, altered it, and called and lured the doctor to an isolated spot they'd chosen. Emil the Terrible, a heavy club in hand, crouched in the shadows across the street from 6438 North Whipple. Nash stood at the entrance, and Goethe, gun in hand, hid behind a tree nearby. Livingston was the wheel man, parked half a block north.

Peacock drove up and got out of his car, medical bag in hand. Bobby stuck the gun in the doctor's back and told him not to move. Peacock was led a block north after Emil the Terrible had smacked him "a lick for luck." At this point Peacock fought back, wrestling with Bobby, who shot the doctor in the head. Peacock dropped to the ground, and Emil the Imbecilic hit the dead man again and again with the club. A scalpel from the medical bag in one hand, the gun held butt forward in the other, Bobby added some finishing touches. Nash pulled up in the doctor's car, Livingston following. The corpse was then tossed in the backseat of the Caddy, which was abandoned three blocks away.

Total take for the daring boys: twenty dollars. Just what I'd made on the case, only they didn't get five bucks expenses.

What Bobby, Emil and Nash did get was 199 years plus consecutive terms of one year to life on four robbery counts. Little Mickey was given a thirty-year sentence, and was eventually paroled. The others, to the best of my knowledge, never were.

Ruth Peacock moved to Quincy, Illinois, where she devoted the rest of her life to social service, her church and Red Cross work, as well as to raising her two daughters, Betty Lou and Nancy. Nancy never knew her father.

Maybe that's why Ruth Peacock was so convinced of her husband's loyalty, despite the mysterious circumstances of his death.

She was pregnant with his child at the time.

MARBLE MILDRED

IN JUNE 1936, CHICAGO WAS IN THE MIDST
of the Great Depression and a sweltering
summer, and I was in the midst of Chicago. Specifically, on
this Tuesday afternoon, the ninth to be exact, I was sitting on
a sofa in the minuscule lobby of the Van Buren Hotel. The sofa
had seen better days, and so had the hotel. The Van Buren was
no flophouse, merely a moderately rundown residential hotel
just west of the El tracks, near the LaSalle Street Station.

Divorce work wasn't the bread and butter of the A-1
Detective Agency, but we didn't turn it away. I use the
editorial "we," but actually there was only one of us, me,
Nathan Heller, "president" of the firm. And despite my high-
flown title, I was just a down-at-the-heels dick reading a racing
form in a seedy hotel's seedy lobby, waiting to see if a certain
husband showed up in the company of another woman.

An other woman, that is, than the one he was married to, the
dumpy, dusky dame who'd come to my office yesterday.

"I'm not as good-looking as I was fourteen years ago,"
she'd said, coyly, her voice honeyed by a southern drawl, "but
I'm a darn sight younger looking than *some* women I know."

"You're a very handsome woman, Mrs. Bolton," I said, smiling, figuring she was fifty if she was a day, "and I'm sure there's nothing to your suspicions."

She had been a looker once, but she'd run to fat, and her badly hennaed hair and overdone make-up were no help; nor was the raccoon stole she wore over a faded floral-print housedress. The stole looked a bit ratty and in any case was hardly called for in this weather.

"Mr. Heller, they are more than suspicions. My husband is a successful businessman, with an office in the financial district. He is easy prey to gold diggers."

The strained formality of her tone made the raccoon stole make sense, somehow.

"This isn't the first time you've suspected him of infidelity."

"Unfortunately, no."

"Are you hoping for reconciliation, or has a lawyer advised you to establish grounds for divorce?"

"At this point," she said, calmly, the southern drawl making her words seem more casual than they were, "I wish only to know. Can you understand that, Mr. Heller?"

"Certainly. I'm afraid I'll need some details . . ."

She had them. Though they lived in Hyde Park, a quiet, quietly well-off residential area, Bolton was keeping a room at the Van Buren Hotel, a few blocks down the street from the very office in which we sat. Mrs. Bolton believed that he went to the hotel on assignations while pretending to leave town on business trips.

"How did you happen to find that out?" I asked her.

"His secretary told me," she said, with a crinkly little smile, proud of herself.

"Are you sure you need a detective? You seem to be doing pretty well on your own . . ."

The smile disappeared and she seemed quite serious now, digging into her big black purse and coming back with a folded wad of cash. She thrust it across the desk toward me, as if daring me to take it.

I don't take dares, but I do take money. And there was plenty of it: a hundred in tens and fives.

"My rate's ten dollars a day and expenses," I said, reluctantly, the notion of refusing money going against the grain. "A thirty-dollar retainer would be plenty . . ."

She nodded curtly. "I'd prefer you accept that. But it's all I can afford, remember; when it's gone, it's gone."

I wrote her out a receipt and told her I hoped to refund some of the money, though of course I hoped the opposite, and that I hoped to be able to dispel her fears about her husband's fidelity, though there was little hope of that, either. Hope was in short supply in Chicago, these days.

Right now, she said, Joe was supposedly on a business trip; but the secretary had called to confide in Mrs. Bolton that her husband had been in the office all day.

I had to ask the usual questions. She gave me a complete description (and a photo she'd had the foresight to bring), his business address, working hours, a list of places he was known to frequent.

And, so, I had staked out the hotel yesterday, starting late afternoon. I didn't start in the lobby. The hotel was a walk-up, the lobby on the second floor, the first floor leased out to a saloon, in the window of which I sat nursing beers and watching people stroll by. One of them, finally, was Joseph Bolton, a tall, nattily attired businessman about ten years his wife's junior; he was pleasant looking, but with his wire-rimmed glasses and receding brown hair was no Robert Taylor.

Nor was he enjoying feminine company, unless said company was already up in the hotel room before I'd arrived on the scene. I followed him up the stairs across the glorified landing of a lobby, where I paused at the desk while he went on up the next flight of stairs to his room—there were no elevators in the Van Buren—and, after buying a newspaper from the desk clerk, went up to Bolton's floor, the third of the four-story hotel, and watched from around a corner as he entered his room.

Back down in the lobby, I approached the desk clerk, an older guy with rheumy eyes and a blue bow tie. I offered him a buck for the name of the guest in room 3C.

"Bolton," he said.

"You're kidding," I said. "Let me see the register." I hadn't bothered coming in earlier to bribe a look because I figured Bolton would be here under an assumed name.

"What's it worth to you?" he asked.

" I already paid," I said, and turned his register around and looked in it. Joseph Bolton it was. Using his own goddamn name. That was a first.

"Any women?" I asked.

"Not that I know of," he said.

"Regular customer?"

"He's been living here a couple months."

"Living here? He's here every night?"

"I dunno. He pays his six bits a day, is all I know. I don't tuck him in."

I gave the guy half a buck to let me rent his threadbare sofa. Sat for another couple of hours and followed two women upstairs. Both seemed to be hookers; neither stopped at Bolton's room.

At a little after eight, Bolton left the hotel and I followed him over to Adams Street, to the Berghoff, the best German restaurant for the money in the Loop. What the hell—I hadn't eaten yet either. We both dined alone.

That night I phoned Mrs. Bolton with my report, such as it was.

"He has a woman in his room," she insisted.

"It's possible," I allowed.

"Stay on the job," she said, and hung up.

I stayed on the job. That is, the next afternoon I returned to the Van Buren Hotel, or anyway to the saloon underneath it, and drank beers and watched the world go by. Now and then the world would go up the hotel stairs. Men I ignored; women that looked like hookers I ignored. One woman, who showed up around four-thirty, I did not ignore.

She was as slender and attractive a woman as Mildred Bolton was not, though she was only a few years younger. And her wardrobe was considerably more stylish than my client's— high-collared white dress with a bright, colorful figured print, white gloves, white shoes, a felt hat with a wide turned-down brim.

She did not look like the sort of woman who would be stopping in at the Van Buren Hotel; but stop in she did.

So did I. I trailed her up to the third floor, where she was met at the door of Bolton's room by a male figure. I just got a glimpse of the guy, but he didn't seem to be Bolton. She went inside.

I used a pay phone in the saloon downstairs and called Mrs. Bolton in Hyde Park.

"I can be there in forty minutes," she said.

"What are you talking about?"

"I want to catch them together. I'm going to claw that hussy's eyes out."

"Mrs. Bolton, you don't want to do that . . ."

"I most certainly do. You can go home, Mr. Heller. You've done your job, and nicely."

And she had hung up.

I had mentioned to her that the man in her husband's room did not seem to be her husband; but that apparently didn't matter. Now I had a choice: I could walk back up to my office and write Mrs. Bolton out a check refunding seventy of her hundred dollars, goddamn it (ten bucks a day, ten bucks expenses—she'd pay for my bribes and beers).

Or I could do the Christian thing and wait around and try to defuse this thing before it got even uglier.

I decided to do the latter. Not because it was the Christian thing—I wasn't a Christian, after all—but because I might be able to convince Mrs. Bolton she needed a few more days' work out of me, to figure out what was really going on here. It seemed to me she could use a little more substantial information, if a divorce was to come out of this. It also seemed to me I could use the money.

I don't know how she arrived—whether by El or streetcar or bus or auto—but as fast as she was walking, it could've been on foot. She was red in the face, eyes hard and round as marbles, fists churning as she strode, her head floating above the incongruous raccoon stole.

I hopped off my bar stool and caught her at the sidewalk.

"Don't go in there, Mrs. Bolton," I said, taking her arm gently.

She swung it away from me, held her head back and, short as she was, looked down at me, nostrils flared. I felt like a matador who dropped his cape.

"You've been discharged for the day, Mr. Heller," she said.

"You still need my help. You're not going about this the right way."

With indignation she began, "My husband . . ."

"Your husband isn't in there. He doesn't even get off work till six."

She swallowed. The redness of her face seemed to fade some; I was quieting her down.

Then fucking fate stepped in, in the form of that swanky dame in the felt hat, who picked that very moment to come strolling out of the Van Buren Hotel, like it was the goddamn Palmer House. On her arm was a young man, perhaps eighteen, perhaps twenty, in a cream-color seersucker suit and a gold tie with a pale complexion and sky-blue eyes and cornsilk blond hair; he and the woman on his arm shared the same sensitive mouth.

"Whore!" somebody shouted.

Who else? My client.

I put my hand over my face and shook my head and wished I was dead, or at least in my office.

"Degenerate!" Mrs. Bolton sang out. She rushed toward the slender woman, who reared back, properly horrified. The young man gripped the woman's arm tightly; whether to protect her or himself, it wasn't quite clear.

Well, the sidewalks were filled with people who'd gotten off work, heading for the El or the LaSalle Street Station, so we had an audience. Yes we did.

And Mrs. Bolton was standing nose to nose with the startled woman, saying defiantly, "I am *Mrs.* Bolton—you've been up to see my husband!"

"Why, Mrs. Bolton," the woman said, backing away as best she could. "Your husband is not in his room."

"Liar!"

"If he were in the room, I wouldn't have been in there myself, I assure you."

"Lying whore . . ."

"Okay," I said, wading in, taking Mrs. Bolton by the arm, less gently this time, "that's enough."

"Don't talk to my mother that way," the young man said to Mrs. Bolton.

"I'll talk to her any way I like, you little degenerate."

And the young man slapped my client. It was a loud, ringing slap and drew blood from one corner of her wide mouth.

I pointed a finger at the kid's nose. "That wasn't nice. Back away."

My client's eyes were glittering; she was smiling, a blood-flecked smile that wasn't the sanest thing I ever saw. Despite the gleeful expression, she began to scream things at the couple: "Whore! Degenerate!"

"Oh Christ," I said, wishing I'd listened to my old man and finished college.

We were encircled by a crowd who watched all this with bemused interest, some people smiling, others frowning, others frankly amazed. In the street the clop-clop of an approaching mounted police officer, interrupted in the pursuit of parking violators, cut through the din. A tall, lanky officer, he climbed off his mount and pushed through the crowd.

"What's going on here?" he asked.

"This little degenerate hit me," my client said, wearing her bloody mouth and her righteous indignation like medals, and she grabbed the kid by the tie and yanked the poor son of a bitch by it, jerking him silly.

It made me laugh. It was amusing only in a sick way, but I was sick enough to appreciate it.

"That'll be all of that," the officer said. "Now what happened here?"

I filled him in, in a general way, while my client interrupted with occasional non sequiturs; the mother and son just stood there looking chagrined about being the center of attention for perhaps a score of onlookers.

"I want that dirty little brute arrested," Mrs. Bolton said, through an off-white picket fence of clenched teeth. "I'm a victim of assault!"

The poor shaken kid was hardly a brute, and he was cleaner than most, but he admitted having struck her, when the officer asked him.

"I'm going to have to take you in, son," the officer said.

The boy looked like he might cry. Head bowed, he shrugged and his mother, eyes brimming with tears herself, hugged him.

The officer went to a call box and summoned a squad car and soon the boy was sent away, the mother waiting pitifully at the curb as the car pulled off, the boy's pale face looking back, a sad cameo in the window.

I was at my client's side.

"Let me help you get home, Mrs. Bolton," I said, taking her arm again.

She smiled tightly, patronizingly, withdrew her arm. "I'm fine, Mr. Heller. I can take care of myself. I thank you for your assistance."

And she rolled like a tank through what remained of the crowd, toward the El station.

I stood there a while, trying to gather my wits; it would have taken a better detective than yours truly to find them, however, so, finally, I approached the shattered woman who still stood at the curb. The crowd was gone. So was the mounted officer. All that remained were a few horse apples and me.

"I'm sorry about all that," I told her.

She looked at me, her face smooth, her eyes sad; they were a darker blue than her son's. "What's your role in this?"

"I'm an investigator. Mrs. Bolton suspects her husband of infidelity."

She laughed harshly—a very harsh laugh for such a refined woman. "My understanding is that Mrs. Bolton has suspected that for some fourteen years—and without foundation. But at this point, it would seem moot, one would think."

"Moot? What are you talking about?"

"The Boltons have been separated for months. Mr. Bolton is suing her for divorce."

"What? Since when?"

"Why, since January."

"Then Bolton *does* live at the Van Buren Hotel, here?"

"Yes. My brother and I have known Mr. Bolton for years. My son Charles came up to Chicago recently, to find work, and Joe—Mr. Bolton—is helping him find a job."

"You're, uh, not from Chicago?"

"I live in Woodstock. I'm a widow. Have you any other questions?"

"Excuse me, ma'am. I'm sorry about this. Really. My client misled me about a few things." I tipped my hat to her.

She warmed up a bit; gave me a smile. Tentative, but a smile. "Your apology is accepted, mister . . . ?"

"Heller," I said. "Nathan. And your name?"

"Marie Winston," she said, and extended her gloved hand. I grasped it, smiled.

"Well," I said, shrugged, smiled, tipped my hat again and headed back for my office.

It wasn't the first time a client had lied to me, and it sure wouldn't be the last. But I'd never been lied to in quite this way. For one thing, I wasn't sure Mildred Bolton knew she *was* lying. This lady clearly did not have all her marbles.

I put the hundred bucks in the bank and the matter out of my mind, until I received a phone call, on the afternoon of June 14.

"This is Marie Winston, Mr. Heller. Do you remember me?"

At first, frankly, I didn't; but said, "Certainly. What can I do for you, Mrs. Winston?"

"That . . . incident out in front of the Van Buren Hotel last Wednesday, which you witnessed . . . "

"Oh yes. What about it?"

"Mrs. Bolton has insisted on pressing charges. I wonder if you could appear in police court tomorrow morning and explain what happened?"

"Well . . ."

"Mr. Heller, I would greatly appreciate it."

I don't like turning down attractive women, even on the telephone; but there was more to it than that: the emotion in her voice got to me.

"Well, sure," I said.

So the next morning I headed over to the south Loop police court and spoke my piece. I kept to the facts, which I felt would pretty much exonerate all concerned. The circumstances were, as they say, extenuating.

Mildred Bolton, who glared at me as if I'd betrayed her, approached the bench and spoke of the young man's "unprovoked assault." She claimed to be suffering physically and mentally from the blow she'd received. The latter, at least, was believable. Her eyes were round and wild as she answered the judge's questions.

When the judge fined young Winston one hundred dollars, Mrs. Bolton stood in her place in the gallery and began to clap. The judge looked at her, too startled to rap his gavel and demand order; then she flounced out of the courtroom, very girlishly, tossing her raccoon stole over her shoulder, exulting in her victory.

An embarrassed silence fell across the room. And it's hard to embarrass hookers, a brace of which were awaiting their turn at the docket.

Then the judge pounded his gavel and said, "The court vacates this young man's fine."

Winston, who'd been hangdog throughout the proceedings, brightened like his switch had been turned on; he pumped his lawyer's hand and turned to his mother, seated behind him just beyond the railing, and they hugged.

On the way out Marie Winston, smiling gently, touched my arm and said, "Thank you very much, Mr. Heller."

"I don't think I made much difference."

"I think you did. The judge vacated the fine, after all."

"Hell, I had nothing to do with that. Mildred was your star witness."

"In a way I guess she was."

"I notice her husband wasn't here."

Son Charles spoke up. "No, he's at work. He . . . well, he thought it was better he not be here. We figured *that woman* would be here, after all."

"'That woman' is sick."

"In the head," Charles said bitterly.

"That's right. You or I could be sick that way, too. Somebody ought to help her."

Marie Winston, straining to find some compassion for Mildred Bolton, said, "Who would you suggest?"

"Damn it," I said, "the husband. He's been with her fourteen years. She didn't get this way overnight. The way I see it, he's got a responsibility to get her some goddamn *help* before he dumps her by the side of the road."

Mrs. Winston smiled at that, some compassion coming through after all. "You have a very modern point of view, Mr. Heller."

"Not really. I'm not even used to talkies yet. Anyway, I'll see you, Mrs. Winston. Charles."

And I left the graystone building and climbed in my '32

Auburn and drove back to my office. I parked in the alley in my space, and walked over to the Berghoff for lunch. I think I hoped to find Bolton there. But he wasn't.

I went back to the office and puttered a while; I had a pile of retail credit-risk checks to whittle away at.

Hell with it, I thought, and walked over to Bolton's office building, a narrow, fifteen-story white granite structure just behind the Federal Reserve on West Jackson, next to the El. Bolton was doing all right—better than me, certainly—but as a broker he was in the financial district only by a hair. No doubt he was a relatively small-time insurance broker, making twenty or twenty-five grand a year. Big money by my standards, but a lot of guys over at the Board of Trade spilled more than that.

There was no lobby really, just a wide hall between facing rows of shops, travel agency, cigar store. A uniformed elevator operator, a skinny, pockmarked guy about my age, was waiting for a passenger; I was it.

"Tenth floor," I told him, and he took me up.

He was pulling open the cage doors when we heard the air crack, three times.

"What the hell was that?" he said.

"It wasn't a car backfiring," I said. "You better stay here."

I moved cautiously out into the hall. The elevators came up a central shaft, with a squared-off C of offices all about. I glanced at the names on the pebbled glass in the wood-partition walls, and finally lit upon BOLTON AND SCHMIDT, INSURANCE BROKERS. I swallowed and moved cautiously in that direction as the door flew open and a young woman flew out, a dark-haired dish of maybe twenty with wide eyes and a face drained of blood, her silk stockings flashing as she rushed my way.

She fell into my arms and I said, "Are you wounded?"

"No," she swallowed, "but somebody is."

The poor kid was gasping for air; I hauled her toward the bank of elevators. Even under the strain, I was enjoying the feel and smell of her.

"You wouldn't be Joseph Bolton's secretary, by any chance?" I asked, helping her onto the elevator.

She nodded, eyes still huge.

"Take her down," I told the operator.

And I headed back for that office. It was barely in sight when the door opened again and Joseph Bolton lurched out. He had a gun in his hand. His light brown suitcoat was splotched with blood in several places; so was his right arm. He wasn't wearing his eyeglasses, which made his face seem naked somehow. His expression seemed at once frightened, pained and sorrowful.

He staggered toward me like a child taking its first steps, and I held my arms out to him like daddy. But they were more likely his last steps: he fell to the marble floor and began to writhe, tracing abstract designs in his own blood on the smooth surface.

I moved toward him and he pointed the gun at me, a little .32 revolver. "Stay away! Stay away!"

"Okay, bud, okay," I said.

I heard someone laughing.

A woman.

I looked up and in the doorway, feet planted like a giant surveying a puny world, was dumpy little Mildred, in her floral housedress and raccoon stole. Her mug was split in a big, goofy smile.

"Don't pay any attention to him, Mr. Heller," she said, lightly. "He's just faking."

"He's shot to shit, lady!" I said.

Keeping their distance out of respect and fear were various tenth-floor tenants, standing near their various offices, as if witnessing some strange performance.

"Keep her away from me!" Bolton managed to shout. His mouth was bubbling with blood. His body moved slowly across the marble floor, like a slug, leaving a slimy red trail.

I moved to Mrs. Bolton, stood between her and Bolton. "You just take it easy . . . "

Mrs. Bolton, giggling, peeked out from in back of me. "Look at him, fooling everybody."

"You behave," I told her. Then I called out to a businessman of about fifty near the elevators. I asked him if there were any doctors in the building, and he said yes, and I said then for Christsake go get one.

"Why don't you get up and stop faking?" she said teasingly to her fallen husband, the southern drawl dripping off her words, as she craned her neck around me to see him, like she couldn't bear to miss a moment of the show.

"Keep her away! Keep her away!"

Bolton continued to writhe like a wounded snake, but he kept clutching that gun, and wouldn't let anyone near him. He would cry out that he couldn't breathe, beating his legs against the floor; but he seemed always conscious of his wife's presence. He would move his head so as to keep my body between him and her round, cold, glittering eyes.

"Don't you mind Joe, Mr. Heller. He's just putting on an act."

If so, I had a hunch it was his final performance.

And now he began to scream in pain.

I approached him and he looked at me with tears in his eyes, eyes that bore the confusion of a child in pain, and he relented, allowed me to come close, handed me the gun, like he was offering a gift. I accepted it, by the nose of the thing, and dropped it in my pocket.

"Did you shoot yourself, Mr. Bolton?" I asked him.

"Keep that woman away from me," he managed, lips bloody.

"He's not really hurt," his wife said, mincingly, from the office doorway.

"Did your wife shoot you?"

"Just keep her away . . . "

Two people in white came rushing toward us—a doctor and a nurse—and I stepped aside, but the doctor, a middle-aged, rather heavyset man with glasses, asked if I'd give him a hand. I said sure and pitched in.

Bolton was a big man, nearly two hundred pounds I'd say, and pretty much dead weight; we staggered toward the elevator like drunks. Like Bolton himself had staggered toward me, actually. The nurse tagged along.

So did Mrs. Bolton.

The nurse, young, blond, slender, did her best to keep Mrs. Bolton out of the elevator; but Mrs. Bolton pushed her way through like a fullback. The doctor and I, bracing Bolton, couldn't help out the young nurse.

Bolton, barely conscious, said, "Please . . . please, keep her away."

"Now, now," Mrs. Bolton said, the violence of her entry into the elevator forgotten (by her), standing almost primly now, hands folded over the big black purse, "everything will be all right, dear. You'll see."

Bolton began to moan; the pain it suggested wasn't entirely physical.

On the thirteenth floor, a second doctor met us and took my place hauling Bolton, and I went ahead and opened the door onto a waiting room where patients, having witnessed the doctor and nurse race madly out of the office, were milling about expectantly. The nurse guided the doctors and their burden down a hall into an X-ray room. The nurse shut the door on them and faced Mrs. Bolton with a firm look.

"I'm sorry, Mrs. Bolton, you'll have to wait."

"Is that so?" she said.

"Mrs. Bolton," I said, touching her arm.

She glared at me. "Who invited you?"

I resisted the urge to say, *you did, you fucking cow,* and just stood back while she moved up and down the narrow corridor between the offices and examining rooms, searching for a door that would lead her to her beloved husband. She trundled up and down, grunting, talking to herself, and the nurse looked at me helplessly.

"She *is* the wife," I said, with a facial shrug.

The nurse sighed heavily and went to a door adjacent to the X-ray room and called out to Mrs. Bolton; Mrs. Bolton whirled and looked at her fiercely.

"You can view your husband's treatment from in here," the nurse said.

Mrs. Bolton smiled in tight triumph and drove her taxi cab of a body into the room. I followed her. Don't ask me why.

A wide glass panel looked in on the X-ray room. Mrs. Bolton climbed onto an examination table and got up on her knees and watched the flurry of activity beyond the glass, as her husband lay on a table being attended by the pair of frantic doctors.

"Did you shoot him, Mrs. Bolton?" I asked her.

She frowned but did not look at me. "Are *you* still here?"

"You lied to me, Mrs. Bolton."

"No I didn't. And I didn't shoot him, either."

"What happened in there?"

"I never touched that gun." She was moving her head side to side, like somebody in the bleachers trying to see past the person sitting in front.

"Did your husband shoot himself?"

She made a childishly smug face. "Joe's just faking to get everybody's sympathy. He's not really hurt."

The door opened behind me and I turned to see a police officer step in.

The officer frowned at us, and shook his head as if to say, "Oh no." It was an understandable response: it was the same cop, the mounted officer, who'd come upon the disturbance outside the Van Buren Hotel. Not surprising, really—this part of the Loop was his beat, or anyway his horse's.

He crooked his finger for me to step out in the hall and I did.

"I heard a murder was being committed up on the tenth floor of one-sixty-six," he explained, meaning 166 West Jackson. "Do you know what happened? Did you see it?"

I told him what I knew, which for being on the scene was damned little.

"Did she do it?" the officer asked.

"The gun was in the husband's hand," I shrugged. "Speaking of which . . ."

And I took the little revolver out of my pocket, holding the gun by its nose again.

"What make is this?" the officer said, taking it.

"I don't recognize it."

He read off the side: "Narizmande Eibar Spair. Thirty-two caliber."

"It got the job done."

He held the gun so that his hand avoided the grip; tried to break it open, but couldn't.

"What's wrong with this thing?" he said.

"The trigger's been snapped on empty shells, I'd say."

"What does that mean?"

"It means that after six slugs were gone, the shooter kept shooting. Just once around wouldn't drive the shells into the barrel like that."

"Judas," the officer said.

The X-ray room's door opened and the doctor I'd shared the elevator and Bolton's dead weight with stepped into the hall, bloody and bowed.

"He's dead," the doctor said, wearily. "Choked to death on his own blood, poor bastard."

I said nothing; just glanced at the cop, who shrugged.

"The wife's in there," I said, pointing.

But I was pointing to Mrs. Bolton, who had stepped out into the hall. She was smiling pleasantly.

She said, "You're not going to frighten me about Joe. He's a great big man and as strong as a horse. Of course, I begin to think he ought to go to the hospital this time—for a while."

"Mrs. Bolton," the doctor said, flatly, with no sympathy whatsoever, "your husband is dead."

Like a spiteful child, she stuck out her tongue. "Liar," she said.

The doctor sighed, turned to the cop. "Shall I call the morgue, or would you like the honor?"

"You should make the call, doctor," the officer said.

Mrs. Bolton moved slowly toward the door to the X-ray room, from which the other doctor, his smock blood-spattered, emerged. She seemed to lose her footing, then, and I took her arm yet again. This time she accepted the help. I walked her into the room and she approached the body, stroked its brow with stubby fingers.

"I can't believe he'd go," she said.

From behind me, the doctor said, "He's dead, Mrs. Bolton. Please leave the room."

Still stroking her late husband's brow, she said, "He feels cold. So cold."

She kissed his cheek.

Then she smiled down at the body and patted its head, as one might a sleeping child, and said, "He's got a beautiful head, hasn't he?"

The officer stepped into the room and said, "You'd better come along with me, Mrs. Bolton. Captain Stege wants to talk to you."

"You're making a terrible mistake. I didn't shoot him."

He took her arm; she assumed a regal posture. He asked her if she would like him to notify any relatives or friends.

"I have no relatives or friends," she said, proudly. "I never had anybody or wanted anybody except Joe."

A crowd was waiting on the street. Damn near a mob, and at the forefront were the newshounds, legmen and cameramen alike. Cameras were clicking away as Davis of the *News* and a couple of others blocked the car waiting at the curb to take Mrs. Bolton to the Homicide Bureau. The mounted cop, with her in tow, brushed them and their questions aside and soon the car, with her in it, was inching into the late afternoon traffic. The reporters and photogs began flagging cabs to take quick pursuit, but snide, boyish Davis lingered to ask me a question.

"What were you doing here, Heller?"

"Getting a hangnail looked at up at the doctor's office."

"Fuck, Heller, you got blood all over you!"

I shrugged, lifted my middle finger. "Hell of a hangnail."

He smirked and I smirked and pushed through the crowd and hoofed it back to my office.

I was sitting at my desk, about an hour later, when the phone rang.

"Get your ass over here!"

"Captain Stege?"

"No, Walter Winchell. You were an eyewitness to a homicide, Heller! Get your ass over here!"

The phone clicked in my ear and I shrugged to nobody and got my hat and went over to the First District Station, entering off 11th. It was a new, modern, nondescript high rise; if this was the future, who needed it.

In Stege's clean little office, the clean little cop looked out his black-rimmed, round-lensed glasses at me from behind his desk and said, "Did you see her do it?"

"I told the officer at the scene all about it, Captain."

"You didn't make a statement."

"Get a stenographer in here and I will."

He did and I did.

That seemed to cool the stocky little cop down. He and I had been adversaries once, and were getting along better these days. But there was still a strain.

Thought gripped his doughy, owlish countenance. "How do you read it, Heller?"

"I don't know. He had the gun. Maybe it was suicide."

"Everybody in that building agrees with you. Bolton's been having a lot of trouble with his better half. They think she drove him to suicide, finally. But there's a hitch."

"Yeah?"

"Suicides don't usually shoot themselves five times, two of 'em in the back."

I had to give him that.

"You think she's nuts?" Stege asked.

"Nuttier than a fruitcake."

"Maybe. But that was murder—premeditated."

"Oh, I doubt that, Captain. Don't you know a crime of passion when you see it? Doesn't the unwritten law apply to women as well as men?"

"The answer to your question is yes to the first, and no to the second. You want to see something?"

"Sure."

From his desk he handed me a small slip of paper.

It was a receipt for a gun sold on June 11 by the Hammond Loan Company, Hammond, Indiana, to a Mrs. Sarah Weston.

"That was in her purse," Stege said, smugly. "Along with a powder puff, a hanky and some prayer leaflets."

"And you think Sarah Weston is just a name Mrs. Bolton used to buy the .32 from this pawn shop?"

"Certainly. And that slip—found in a narrow side pocket in the lining of her purse—proves premeditation."

"Does it, Captain?" I said, smiling, standing, hat in hand. "It seems to me premeditation would have warned her to get *rid* of that receipt. But then, what do I know? I'm no cop." From the doorway I said, "Just a detective."

And I left him there to mull that over.

In the corridor, on my way out, Sam Backus buttonholed me.

"Got a minute for a pal, Nate?"

"Sam, if we were pals, I'd see you someplace but in court."

Sam was with the Public Defender's office, and I'd bumped into him from time to time, dating back to my cop days. He was a conscientious and skillful attorney who, in better times, might have had a lucrative private practice; in times like these, he was glad to have a job. Sam's sharp features and receding hairline gave the smallish man a ferret-like appearance; he was similarly intense, too.

"My client says she employed you to do some work for

her," he said, in a rush. "She'd like you to continue . . ."

"Wait a minute, wait a minute—your client? Not Mrs. Mildred Bolton?"

"Yes."

"She's poison. You're on your own."

"She tells me you were given a hundred-dollar retainer."

"Well, that's true, but I figure I earned it."

"She figures you owe her some work, or some dough."

"Sam, she lied to me. She misrepresented herself and her intentions." I was walking out the building and he was staying right with me.

"She's a disturbed individual. And she's maintaining she didn't kill her husband."

"They got her cold." I told him about Stege's evidence.

"It could've been planted," he said, meaning the receipt. "Look, Bolton's secretary was up there, and Mrs. Bolton says he and the girl—an Angela something, sounds like 'who-you'—were having an affair."

"I thought the affair was supposed to be with Marie Winston."

"Her, too. Bolton must've been a real ladies' man. And the Winston woman was up there at that office this afternoon, too, before the shooting."

"Was she there during the shooting, though?"

"I don't know. I need to find out. The Public Defender's office doesn't have an investigative staff, you know that, Nate. And I can't afford to hire anybody, and I don't have the time to do the legwork myself. You owe her some days. Deliver."

He had a point.

I gathered some names from Sam, and the next morning I began to interview the participants.

"An affair with Joe?" Angela Houyoux said. "Why, that's nonsense."

We were in the outer office of BOLTON AND SCHMIDT. She'd given me the nickel tour of the place, one outer office, and two inner ones, the one to the south having been Bolton's. The crime scene told me nothing. Angela, the pretty, twentyish, sweet-smelling dark-haired beauty who'd tumbled into my arms and the elevator yesterday, did.

"I was rather shaken by Mrs. Bolton's behavior at first— and his. But then it became rather matter-of-fact to come to the office and find the glass in the door broken, or Mr. Bolton with his hands cut from taking a knife away from Mrs. Bolton. After a few weeks, I grew quite accustomed to having dictation interrupted while Mr. and Mrs. Bolton scuffled and fought and yelled. Lately they argued about Mrs. Winston a lot."

"How was your relationship with Mrs. Bolton?"

"Spotty, I guess you'd call it. Sometimes she'd seem to think I was interested in her husband. Other times she'd confide in me like a sister. I never said much to her. I'd just jerk my shoulders or just look at her kind of sympathetic. I had the feeling she didn't have anybody else to talk to about this. She'd cry and say her husband was unfaithful—I didn't dare point out they'd been separated for a year and that Mr. Bolton had filed for divorce and all. One time . . . well, maybe I shouldn't say it."

"Say it."

"One time she said she 'just might kill' her husband. She said they never convict a woman for murder in Cook County."

Others in the building at West Jackson told similar tales. Bolton's business partner Schmidt wondered why Bolton bothered to get an injunction to keep his wife out of the office, but then refused to mail her her temporary alimony, giving her a reason to come to the office all the time.

"He would dole out the money, two or three dollars at a time," Schmidt said. "He could have paid her what she had coming for a month, or at least a week—Joe made decent money. It would've got rid of her. Why dole it out?"

The elevator operator I'd met yesterday had a particularly wild yarn.

"Yesterday, early afternoon, Mr. Bolton got on at the ninth floor; he seemed in an awful hurry and said, 'Shoot me up to eleven.' I had a signal to stop at ten, so I made the stop and Mrs. Bolton came charging aboard. Mr. Bolton was right next to me. He kind of hid behind me and said, 'For God's sake, she'll kill us both!' I sort of forced the door closed on her, and she stood there in the corridor and raised her fist and said, 'Goddamnit, I'll fix you!' I guess she meant Bolton, not me."

"Apparently."

"Anyway, I took him up to eleven and he kind of sighed and as he got off he said, 'It's just hell, isn't it?' I said it was a damn shame he couldn't do anything about it."

"This was yesterday."

"Yes, sir. Not long before he was killed."

"Did it occur to you, at the time, it might lead to that?"

"No, sir. It was pretty typical, actually. I helped him escape from her before. And I kept her from getting on the elevator downstairs, sometimes. After all, he had an injunction to keep her from 'molesting him at his place of business,' he said."

Even the heavyset doctor up on thirteen found time for me.

"I think they were *both* sick," he said, rather bitterly I thought.

"What do you mean, doctor?"

"I mean that I've administered more first aid to that man than a battlefield physician. That woman has beaten her husband, cut him with a knife, with a razor, created such commotions and scenes with such regularity that the patrol wagon coming for Mildred is a commonplace occurrence on West Jackson."

"How well did you know Bolton?"

"We were friendly. God knows I spent enough time with him, patching him up. He should've been a much more successful man than he was, you know. She drove him out of one job and another. I never understood him."

"Oh?"

"Well, they live, or lived, in Hyde Park. That's a university neighborhood. Fairly refined, very intellectual, really."

"Was Bolton a scholar?"

"He had bookish interests. He liked having the University of Chicago handy. Now why would a man of his sensibilities endure a violent harridan like Mildred Bolton?"

"In my trade, Doc," I said, "we call that a mystery."

I talked to more people. I talked to a pretty, blonde legal secretary named Peggy O'Reilly who, in 1933, had been employed by Ocean Accident and Guarantee Company where Joseph Bolton Jr. was a business associate.

"His desk was four feet from mine," she said. "But I never went out to dinner with him. There was no social contact whatsoever, but Mrs. Bolton didn't believe that. She came into the office and accused me of—well, called me a 'dirty hussy,' if you must know. I asked her to step out into the hall where we wouldn't attract so much attention, and she did—and proceeded to tear my clothes off me. She tore the clothes off my body, scratched my neck, my face, kicked me, it was horrible. The attention it attracted, oh, oh—several hundred people witnessed the sight; two nice men pulled her off of me. I was badly bruised and out of the office a week. When I came back, Mr. Bolton had been discharged."

A pattern was forming here, one I'd seen before; but usually it was the wife who was battered and yet who somehow endured and even encouraged the twisted union. Only Bolton was a battered husband, a strapping man who never turned physically on his abusing wife; his only punishment had been to withhold that money from her, dole it out a few bucks at a time. That was the only satisfaction, the only revenge, he'd been able to extract.

At the Van Buren Hotel I knocked on the door of what had been Bolton's room. 3C.

Young Charles Winston answered. He looked terrible. Pale as milk, only not near as healthy. Eyes bloodshot. He was in a T-shirt and boxer shorts. The other times I'd seen him he'd been fully and even nattily attired.

"Put some clothes on," I said. "We have to talk."

In the saloon below the hotel we did that very thing.

"Joe was a great guy," he said, eyes brimming with tears. He would have cried into his beer, only he was having a mixed drink. I was picking up the tab, so Mildred Bolton was buying it.

"Is your mother still in town?"

He looked up with sharp curiosity. "No. She's back in Woodstock. Why?"

"She was up at the office shortly before Bolton was killed."

"I know. I was there, too."

"Oh?" Now, that was news.

"We went right over, after the hearing."

"To tell him how it came out?"

"Yes, and to thank him. You see, after that incident out in front, last Wednesday, when they took me off to jail, Mother went to see Joe. They met at the Twelfth Street Bus Depot. She asked him if he would take care of my bail—she could have had her brother do it, but I'd have had to spend the night in jail first." He smiled fondly. "Joe went right over to the police station with the money and got me out."

"That was white of him."

"Sure was. Then we met Mother over at the taproom of the Auditorium Hotel."

Very posh digs; interesting place for folks who lived at the Van Buren to be hanging out.

"Unfortunately, I'd taken time to stop back at the hotel to pick up some packages my mother had left behind. Mrs. Bolton must've been waiting here for me, and she followed me to the Auditorium taproom, where she attacked me with her fists, and told the crowd in no uncertain terms, and in a voice to wake the dead, that my mother was . . ." He shook his head. ". . . 'nothing but a whore'. . . and such. Finally the management ejected her."

"Was your mother in love with Joe?"

He looked at me sharply. "Of course not. They were friendly. That's the extent of it."

"When did you and your mother leave Bolton's office?"

"Yesterday? About one-thirty. Mrs. Bolton was announced as being in the outer office, and we just got the hell out."

"Neither of you lingered."

"No. Are you going to talk to my mother?"

"Probably."

"I wish you wouldn't," he said glumly.

I drank my beer, studying the kid.

"Maybe I won't have to," I said, smiled at him, patted his shoulder, and left.

I met with Public Defender Backus in a small interrogation room at the First District Station.

"Your client is guilty," I said.

I was sitting. He was standing. Pacing.

"The secretary was in the outer office at all times," I said. "In view of other witnesses. The Winstons left around one-thirty. They were seen leaving by the elevator operator on duty."

"One of them could have sneaked back up the stairs . . ."

"I don't think so. Anyway, this meeting ends my participation, other than a report I'll type up for you. I've used up the hundred."

From my notes I read off summaries of the various interviews I'd conducted. He finally sat, sweat beading his brow, eyes slitted behind the glasses.

"She says she didn't do it," he said.

"She says a lot of things. I think you can get her off, anyway."

He smirked. "Are you a lawyer now?"

"No. Just a guy who's been in the thick of this bizarre fucking case since day one."

"I bow to your experience if not expertise."

"You can plead her insane, Sam."

"A very tough defense to pull off, and besides, she won't hear of it. She wants no psychiatrists, no alienists involved."

"You can still get her off."

"How in hell?"

I let some air out. "I'm going to have to talk to her before I say any more. It's going to have to be up to her."

"You can't tell me?"

"You're not my client."

Mildred Bolton was.

And she was ushered into the interrogation room by a matron who then waited outside the door. She wore the same floral-print dress, but the raccoon stole was gone. She smiled faintly upon seeing me, sat across from me.

"You been having fun with the press, Mildred, haven't you?"

"I sure have. They call me 'Marble Mildred.' They think I'm cold."

"They think it's unusual for a widow to joke about her dead husband."

"They're silly people. They asked me the name of my attorney and I said, 'Horsefeathers.'" She laughed. That struck her very funny; she was proud of herself over that witty remark.

"I'm glad you can find something to smile about."

"I'm getting hundreds of letters, you know. Fan mail! They say, you should have killed him whether you did or not. I'm not the only woman wronged in Chicago, you know."

"They've got you dead to rights, Mildred. I've seen some of the evidence. I've talked to the witnesses."

"Did you talk to Mrs. Winston? It was her fault, you know. Her and that . . . that boy."

"You went to see Joe after the boy was fined in court."

"Yes! I called him and told him that the little degenerate had been convicted and fined. Then I asked Joe, did he have any money, because I didn't have anything to eat, and he said yes. So I went to the office and when I got there he tried to give me a check for ten dollars. I said, 'I guess you're going to pay that boy's fine and that's why you haven't any money for me?' He said, 'That's all you're going to get.' And I said, 'Do you mean for a whole *week*? To pay rent out of and eat on?' He said, 'Yes, that's all you get.'"

"He was punishing you."

"I suppose. We argued for about an hour and then he said he had business on another floor—that boy's lawyer is on the ninth floor, you know—and I followed him, chased him to the elevator but he got away. I went back and said to Miss Houyoux, 'He ran away from me.' I waited in his office and in about an hour he came back. I said, 'Joe, I have been your wife for fourteen years and I think I deserve more respect and better treatment than that.' He just leaned back in his chair so cocky and said, 'You know what you are?' And then he said it."

"Said it?"

She swallowed; for the first time, those marble eyes filled with tears. "He said, 'You're just a dirty old bitch.' Then he said it again. Then I said, 'Just a dirty old bitch after fourteen years?' And I pointed the gun at him."

"Where was it?"

"It was on his desk where I put it. It was in a blue box I carried in with me."

"What did you do with it, Mildred?"

"The box?"

"The gun."

"Oh. That. I fired it at him."

I gave her a handkerchief and she dabbed her eyes with it.

"How many times did you fire the gun, Mildred?"

"I don't know. He fell over in his chair and then he got up and came toward me and he said, 'Give me that gun, give me that gun.' I said, 'No, I'm going to finish myself now. Let go of me because my hand is on the trigger!'" Her teeth were clenched. "He struggled with me, and his glasses got knocked off, but he got the gun from my hand and he went out in the hall with it. I followed him, but then I turned and went back in his office. I was going to jump out of the window, but I heard him scream in the hall and I ran to him. The gun was lying beside him and I reached for it but he reached and got it first. I went back in the office."

"Why?"

"To jump out the window, I told you. But I just couldn't leave him. I started to go back out and when I opened the door some people were around. You were one of them, Mr. Heller."

"Where did you get that gun, Mildred?"

"At a pawn shop in Hammond, Indiana."

"To kill Joe?"

"To kill myself."

"But you didn't."

"I'm sorry I didn't. I had plenty of time to do it at home, but I wanted to do it in his office. I wanted to embarrass him that way."

"He was shot in the back, Mildred, twice."

"I don't know about that. Maybe his body turned when I was firing. I don't know. I don't remember."

"You know that the prosecution will not buy your suicide claims."

"They are *not* claims!"

"I know they aren't. But they won't buy them. They'll tell the judge and the jury that your talk of suicide is a clever excuse to get around planning Joe's murder. In other words, that you premeditated the killing and supplied yourself with a gun— and a reason for having a gun."

"I don't know about those things."

"Would you like to walk away from this?"

"Well, of course. I'm not crazy."

Right.

"You can, I think. But it's going to be hard on you. They're going to paint you as a shrew. As a brutal woman who battered her husband. They'll suggest that Bolton was too much of a gentleman for his own good, that he should have struck back at you, physically."

She giggled. "He wasn't such a gentleman."

"Really?"

"He wasn't what you think at all. Not at all."

"What do you mean, Mildred?"

"We were married for fourteen years before he tried to get rid of me. That's a long time."

"It sure is. What is it about your husband that we're getting wrong?"

"I haven't said."

"I know that. Tell me."

"I won't tell you. I've never told a living soul. I never will."

"I think you should. I think you need to."

"I won't. I won't now. I won't ever."

"There were no other women, were there, Mildred?"

"There were countless women, countless!"

"Like Marie Winston."

"She was the worst!"

"What about her son?"

"That little . . ." She stopped herself.

"That little degenerate? That's what you seem to always call him."

She nodded, pursing her thin wide lips.

"Joe was living in a fleabag hotel," I said. "A guy with *his* money. Why?"

"It was close to his work."

"Relatively. I think it had to do with who he was living with. A young man."

"A lot of men room together."

"There were no other women, were there, Mildred? Your husband used you to hide behind, didn't he, for many years."

She was crying now. The marble woman was crying now. "I loved him. I loved him."

"I know you did. And I don't know when you discovered it. Maybe you never did, really. Maybe you just suspected, and couldn't bring yourself to admit it. Then, after he left you, after he moved out of the house, you finally decided to find out, really find out, hiring me, springing for a hundred precious bucks you'd scrimped and saved, knowing I might find things out you'd want kept quiet. Knowing I might confirm the suspicions that drove you bughouse for years."

"Stop it . . . please stop it . . ."

"Your refined husband who liked to be near a college campus. You knew there were affairs. And there were. But not with women."

She stood, squeezing my hanky in one fist. "I don't have to listen to this!"

"You do if you want to be a free woman. The unwritten law doesn't seem to apply for women as equally as it does for men. But if you tell the truth about your husband—about just who it was he was seeing behind your back—I guarantee you no jury will convict you."

Her mouth was trembling.

I stood. "It's up to you, Mildred."

"Are you going to tell Mr. Backus?"

"No. You're my client. I'll respect your wishes."

"I wish you would just go. Just go, Mr. Heller."

I went.

I told Backus nothing except that I would suggest he introduce expert testimony from an alienist. He didn't. His client wouldn't hear of it.

The papers continued to have a great time with Marble Mildred. She got to know the boys of the press, became bosom buddies with the sob sisters, warned cameramen not to take a profile pic or she'd break their lens, shouted greetings and wisecracks to one and all. She laughed and talked; being on trial for murder was a lark for her.

Of course as the trial wore on, she grew less boisterous, even became sullen at times; on the stand she told her story more or less straight, but minus any hint her husband was bent.

The prosecution, as I had told her they would, ridiculed her statement that she'd bought the .32 to do herself in. The prosecutor extolled "motherhood and wifehood," but expressed "the utmost contempt for Mildred Bolton." She was described as "dirt," "filth," "vicious," and more. She was sentenced to die in the electric chair.

She didn't want an appeal, a new trial.

"As far as I am concerned," she told the stunned judge, "I am perfectly satisfied with things as they now stand."

But Cook County was squeamish about electrocuting a woman; just half an hour before the execution was to take place, hair shaved above one ear, wearing special females-only electrocution shorts, Mildred was spared by Governor Horner.

Mildred, who'd been strangely blissful in contemplation of her electrocution, was less pleased with her new sentence of 199 years. Nonetheless she was a model prisoner, until August 29, 1943, when she was found slumped in her cell, wrists slashed. She had managed to smuggle some scissors in. It took her hours to die. Sitting in the darkness, waiting for the blood to empty out of her.

She left a note, stuck to one wall: "To whom it may concern. In the event of my death do not notify anybody or try to get in touch with family or friends. I wish to die as I have lived, completely alone."

What she said was true, but I wondered if I was the only person alive who knew that it hadn't been by choice.

THE
STRAWBERRY
TEARDROP

I N A GARBAGE DUMP ON EAST NINTH STREET near Shore Drive, in Cleveland, Ohio, on August 17, 1938, a woman's body was discovered by a cop walking his morning beat.

I got there before anything much had been moved. Not that I was a plainclothes dick—I used to be, but not in Cleveland; I was just along for the ride. I'd been sitting in the office of Cleveland's Public Safety Director, having coffee, when the call came through. The Safety Director was in charge of both the police and fire departments, and one would think that a routine murder wouldn't rate a call to such a high muckey-muck.

One would be wrong.

Because this was the latest in a series of anything-but-routine, brutal murders—the unlucky thirteenth, to be exact, not that the thirteenth victim would seem any more unlucky than the preceding twelve. The so-called "Mad Butcher of Kingsbury Run" had been exercising his ghastly art sporadically since the fall of '35, in Cleveland—or so I understood. I was an out-of-towner, myself.

So was the woman.

Or she used to be, before she became so many dismembered parts flung across this rock-and-garbage strewn dump. Her nude torso was slashed and the blood, splashed here, streaked there, was turning dark, almost black, though the sun caught scarlet glints and tossed them at us. Her head was gone, but maybe it would turn up. The Butcher wasn't known for that, though. The twelve preceding victims had been found headless, and had stayed that way. Somewhere in Cleveland, perhaps, a guy had a collection in his attic. In this weather it wouldn't smell too nice.

It's not a good sign when the Medical Examiner gets sick; and the half dozen cops, and the police photographer, were looking green around the gills themselves. Only my friend, the Safety Director, seemed in no danger of losing his breakfast. He was a ruddy-cheeked six-footer in a coat and tie and vest, despite the heat; hatless, his hair brushed back and pomaded, he still seemed—years after I'd met him—boyish. And he was only in his mid-thirties, just a few years older than me.

I'd met him in Chicago, seven or eight years ago, when I wasn't yet president (and everything else) of the A-1 Detective Agency, but still a cop; and he was still a Prohibition Agent. Hell, *the* Prohibition Agent. He'd considered me one of the more or less honest cops in Chicago—emphasis on the less, I guess—and I made a good contact for him, as a lot of the cops didn't like him much. Honesty doesn't go over real big in Chicago, you know.

Eliot Ness said, "Despite the slashing, there's a certain skill displayed, here."

"Yeah, right," I said. "A regular ballet dancer did this."

"No, really," he said, and bent over the headless torso, pointing. He seemed to be pointing at the gathering flies, but he wasn't. "There's an unmistakable precision about this.

Maybe even indicating surgical training."

"Maybe," I said. "But I think the doctor lost this patient."

He stood and glanced at me and smiled, just a little; he understood me: he knew my wise-guy remarks were just my way of holding onto my own breakfast.

"You ought to come to Cleveland more often," he said.

"You know how to show a guy a good time, I'll give you that, Eliot."

He walked over and glanced at a forearm, which seemed to reach for an empty soap box, fingers stretched toward the Gold Dust twins. He knelt and studied it.

I wasn't here on a vacation, by any means. Cleveland didn't strike me as a vacation city, even before I heard about the Butcher of Kingsbury Run (so-called because a number of the bodies, including the first several, were found in that Cleveland gulley). This was strictly business. I was here trying to trace the missing daughter of a guy in Evanston who owned a dozen diners around Chicago. He was one of those self-made men, who started out in the greasy kitchen of his own first diner, fifteen or so years ago; and now he had a fancy brick house in Evanston and plenty of money, considering the times. But not much else. His wife had died four or five years ago, of consumption; and his daughter—who he claimed to be a good girl and by all other accounts was pretty wild—had wandered off a few months ago, with a taxi dancer from the North Side named Tony.

Well, I'd found Tony in Toledo—he was doing a floor show in a roadhouse with a dark-haired girl named FiFi; he'd grown a little pencil mustache and they did an Apache routine—he was calling himself Antoine now. And Tony/Antoine said Ginger (which was the Evanston restauranteur's daughter's nickname) had taken up with somebody named Ray, who owned (get this) a diner in Cleveland.

I'd gotten here yesterday, and had talked to Ray, and without tipping I was looking for her, asked where was the pretty waitress, the one called Ginger, I think her name is. Ray, a skinny, balding guy of about thirty with a silver front tooth, leered and winked and made it obvious that not only was Ginger working as a waitress here, she was also a side dish, where Ray was concerned. Further casual conversation revealed that it was Ginger's night off—she was at the movies with some girlfriends—and she'd be in tomorrow, around five.

I didn't push it further, figuring to catch up with her at the diner the next evening, after wasting a day seeing Cleveland and bothering my old friend Eliot. And now I was in a city dump with him, watching him study the severed forearm of a woman.

"Look at this," Eliot said, pointing at the outstretched fingers of the hand.

I went over to him and it—not quickly, but I went over.

"What, Eliot? Do you want to challenge my powers of deduction, or just make me sick?"

"Just a lucky break," he said. "Most of the victims have gone unidentified; too mutilated. And a lot of 'em have been prostitutes or vagrants. But we've got a break, here. Two breaks, actually."

He pointed to the hand's little finger. To the small, gold filigree band with a green stone.

"A nice specific piece of jewelry to try to trace," he said, with a dry smile. "And even better . . ."

He pointed to a strawberry birthmark, the shape of a teardrop, just below the wrist.

I took a close look; then stood. Put a hand on my stomach.

Walked away and dropped to my knees and lost my breakfast.

I felt Eliot's hand patting my back.

"Nate," he said. "What's the matter? You've seen homicides before . . . even grisly ones like this . . . brace up, boy."

He eased me to my feet.

My tongue felt thick in my mouth, thick and restless.

"What is it?" he said.

"I think I just found my client's daughter," I said.

Both the strawberry birthmark and the filigree ring with the green stone had been part of my basic description of the girl; the photographs I had showed her to be a pretty but average-looking young woman—slim, brunette—who resembled every third girl you saw on the street. So I was counting on those two specifics to help me identify her. I hadn't counted on those specifics helping me in just this fashion.

I sat in Eliot's inner office in the Cleveland city hall; the mayor's office was next door. We were having coffee with some rum in it—Eliot kept a bottle in a bottom drawer of his rolltop desk. I promised him not to tell Capone.

"I think we should call the father," Eliot said. "Ask him to come and make the identification."

I thought about it. "I'd like to argue with you, but I don't see how I can. Maybe if we waited till . . . Christ. Till the head turns up . . ."

Eliot shrugged. "It isn't likely to. The ring and the birthmark are enough to warrant notifying the father."

"I can make the call."

"No. I'll let you talk to him when I'm done, but that's something I should do."

And he did. With quiet tact. After a few minutes he handed me the phone; if I'd thought him cold at the scene of the crime, I erased that thought when I saw the dampness in the gray eyes.

"Is it my little girl?" the deep voice said, sounding tinny out of the phone.

"I think so, Mr. Jensen. I'm afraid so."

I could hear him weeping.

Then he said: "Mr. Ness said her body was . . . dismembered. How can you say it's her? How . . . how can you know it's her?"

And I told him of the ring and the strawberry teardrop.

"I should come there," he said.

"Maybe that won't be necessary." I covered the phone. "Eliot, will my identification be enough?"

He nodded. "We'll stretch it."

I had to argue with Jensen, but finally he agreed for his daughter's remains to be shipped back via train; I said I'd contact a funeral home this afternoon, and accompany her home.

I handed the phone to Eliot to hang up.

We looked at each other and Eliot, not given to swearing, said, "I'd give ten years of my life to nail that butchering bastard."

"How long will your people need the body?"

"I'll speak to the coroner's office. I'm sure we can send her home with you in a day or two. Where are you staying?"

"The Stadium Hotel."

"Not anymore. I've got an extra room for you. I'm a bachelor again, you know."

We hadn't gotten into that yet; I'd always considered Eliot's marriage an ideal one, and was shocked a few months back to hear it had broken up.

"I'm sorry, Eliot."

"Me too. But I am seeing somebody. Someone you may remember; another Chicagoan."

"Who?"

"Evie MacMillan."

"The fashion illustrator? Nice looking woman."

Eliot smiled slyly. "You'll see her tonight, at the Country Club . . . but I'll arrange some female companionship for you. I don't want you cutting my time."

"How can you say such a thing? Don't you trust me?"

"I learned a long time ago," he said, turning to his desk full of paperwork, "not to trust Chicago cops—even ex-ones."

Out on the Country Club terrace, the ten-piece band was playing Cole Porter and a balmy breeze from Lake Erie was playing with the women's hair. There were plenty of good-looking women, here—low-cut dresses, bare shoulders—and lots of men in evening clothes for them to dance with. But this was no party, and since some of the golfers were still here from late afternoon rounds, there were sports clothes and a few business suits (like mine) in the mix. Even some of the women were dressed casually, like the tall, slender blonde in a pink shirt and pale green pleated skirt who sat down next to me at the little white metal table and asked me if I'd have a Bacardi with her. The air smelled like a flower garden, and some of it was flowers, and some of it was her.

"I'd be glad to buy you a Bacardi," I said, clumsily.

"No," she said, touching my arm. She had eyes the color of jade. "You're a guest. I'll buy."

Eliot was dancing with his girl Evie, an attractive brunette in her mid-thirties; she'd always struck me as intelligent but sad, somehow. They smiled over at me.

The blonde in pink and pale green brought two Bacardis over, set one of them in front of me and smiled. "Yes," she said wickedly. "You've been set up. I'm the girl Eliot promised you. But if you were hoping for somebody in an evening gown, I'm not it. I just *had* to get an extra nine holes in."

"If you were looking for a guy in a tux," I said, "I'm not it.

And I've never been on a golf course in my life. What else do we have in common?"

She had a nicely wry smile, which continued as she sipped the Bacardi. "Eliot, I suppose. If I have a few more of these, I may tell you a secret."

And after a few more, she did.

And it was a whopper.

"*You're* an undercover agent?" I said. A few sheets to the wind myself.

"Shhhh," she said, finger poised uncertainly before pretty lips. "It's a secret. But I haven't been doing it much lately."

"Haven't been doing what?"

"Well, undercover work. And there's a double entendre there that I'd rather you didn't go looking for."

"I wouldn't think of looking under the covers for it."

The band began playing a tango.

I asked her how she got involved, working for Eliot. Which I didn't believe for a second, even in my cups.

But it turned out to be true (as Eliot admitted to me when he came over to see how Vivian and I were getting along, when Vivian—which was her name, incidentally—went to the powder room with Evie).

Vivian Chalmers was the daughter of a banker (a solvent one), a divorcée of thirty with no children and a lot of social pull. An expert trapshooter, golfer, tennis player and "all 'round sportswoman," with a sense of adventure. When Eliot called on her to case various of the gambling joints he planned to raid—as a socialite she could take a fling in any joint she chose, without raising any suspicion—she immediately said yes. And she'd been an active agent in the first few years of Eliot's ongoing battle against the so-called Mayfield Road Mob,which controlled prostitution, gambling and the policy racket in the Cleveland environs.

"But things have slowed down," she said, nostalgically. "Eliot has pretty much cleaned up the place, and, besides, he doesn't want to use me anymore."

"An undercover agent can only be effective so long," I said. "Pretty soon the other side gets suspicious."

She shrugged, with resigned frustration, and let me buy the next round.

We took a walk in the dark, around the golf course, and ended up sitting on a green. The breeze felt nice. The flag on the hole—13—flapped.

"Thirteen," I said.

"Huh?"

"Victim thirteen. "

"Oh. Eliot told me about that. Your 'luck' today, finding your client's missing daughter. Damn shame."

"Damn shame."

"A shame, too, they haven't found the son-of-a-bitch."

She was a little drunk, and so was I, but I was still shocked—well, amused—to hear a woman, particularly a "society" woman, speak that way.

"It must grate on Eliot, too," I said.

"Sure as hell does. It's the only mote in his eye. He's a hero around these parts, and he's kicked the Mayfield Mob in the seat of the pants, and done everything else from clean up a corrupt police department to throw labor racketeers in jail, to cut traffic deaths in half, to founding Boy's Town, to . . ."

"You're not in love with the guy, are you?"

She seemed taken aback for a minute, then her face wrinkled into a got-caught-with-my-pants-down grin. "Maybe a little. But he's got a girl."

"I don't."

"You might."

She leaned forward.

We kissed for a while, and she felt good in my arms; she was firm, almost muscular. But she smelled like flowers. And the sky was blue and scattered with stars above us, as we lay back on the golf green to look up. It seemed like a nice world, at the moment.

Hard to imagine it had a Butcher in it.

I sat up talking with Eliot that night; he lived in a little reconverted boathouse on the lake. The furnishings were sparse, spartan—it was obvious his wife had taken most of the furniture with her and he'd had to all but start over.

I told him I thought Vivian was a terrific girl.

Leaning back in a comfy chair, feet on an ottoman, Eliot, tie loose around his neck, smiled in a melancholy way. "I thought you'd hit it off."

"Did you have an affair with her?"

He looked at me sharply; that was about as personal as I'd ever got with him.

He shook his head no, but I didn't quite buy it.

"You knew Evie MacMillan in Chicago," I said.

"Meaning what?"

"Meaning nothing."

"Meaning I knew her when I was still married."

"Meaning nothing."

"Nate, I'm sorry I'm not the Boy Scout you think I am."

"Hey, so you've slept with girls before. I'll learn to live with it."

There was a stone fireplace in which some logs were trying to decide whether to burn anymore or not; we watched them trying.

"I love Evie, Nate. I'm going to marry her."

"Congratulations."

We could hear the lake out there; could smell it some, too.

"I'd like that bastard's neck in my hands," Eliot said.

"What?"

"That Butcher. That goddamn Butcher."

"What made you think of him?"

"I don't know."

"Eliot, it's been over three years since he first struck, and you *still* don't have anything?"

"Nothing. A few months ago, last time he hit, we found some of the . . . body parts, bones and such . . . in a cardboard box in the Central Market area. There's a Hooverville over there, or what used to be a Hooverville . . . it's a shantytown, is more like it, genuine hobos as opposed to just good folks down on their luck. Most of the victims—before today—were either prostitutes or bums . . . and the bums from that shanty-town were the Butcher's meat. So to speak."

The fire crackled.

Eliot continued: "I decided to make a clean sweep. I took twenty-five cops through there at one in the morning, and rousted out all the 'bo's and took 'em down and fingerprinted and questioned all of 'em."

"And it amounted to . . . ?"

"It amounted to nothing. Except ridding Cleveland of that shantytown. I burned the place down that afternoon."

"Comes in handy, having all those firemen working for you. But what about those poor bastards whose 'city' you burned down?"

Sensing my disapproval, he glanced at me and gave me what tried to be a warm smile, but was just a weary one.

"Nate, I turned them over to the Relief Department, for relocation and, I hope, rehabilitation. But most of them were bums who just hopped a freight out. And I did 'em a favor by taking them off the potential victims list."

"And made room for Ginger Jensen."

Eliot looked away.

"That wasn't fair," I said. "I'm sorry I said that, Eliot."

"I know, Nate. I know."

But I could tell he'd been thinking the same thing.

I had lunch the next day with Vivian in a little outdoor restaurant in the shadow of Terminal Tower. We were served lemonade and little ham and cheese and lettuce and tomato sandwiches with the crusts trimmed off the toasted bread. The detective in me wondered what became of the crusts.

"Thanks for having lunch with me," Vivian said. She had on a pale orange dress; she sat crossing her brown pretty legs.

"My pleasure," I said.

"Speaking of which . . . about last night . . ."

"We were both a little drunk. Forget it. Just don't ask me to."

She smiled as she nibbled her sandwich.

"I called and told Eliot something this morning," she said, "and he just ignored me."

"What was that?"

"That I have a possible lead on the Butcher murders."

"I can't imagine Eliot ignoring that . . . and it's not like it's just *anybody* approaching him—you *did* work for him . . ."

"Not lately. And he thinks I'm just . . ."

"Looking for an excuse to be around him?"

She nibbled at a little sandwich. Nodded.

"Did you resent him asking you to be with me as a blind date last night?"

"No," she said.

"Did . . . last night have anything to do with wanting to 'show' Eliot?"

If she weren't so sophisticated—or trying to be—she would've looked hurt; but her expression managed to get something else across: disappointment in me.

"Last night had to do with showing *you,*" she said. "And . . . it had a little to do with Bacardi rum . . ."

"That it did. Tell me about your lead."

"Eliot has been harping on the 'professional' way the bodies have been dismembered—he's said again and again he sees a 'surgical' look to it."

I nodded.

"So it occurred to me that a doctor—anyway, somebody who'd at least been in medical school for a time—would be a likely candidate for the Butcher."

"Yes."

"And medical school's expensive, so, it stands to reason, the Butcher just might run in the same social circles as yours truly."

"Say, you *did* work for Eliot."

She liked that.

She continued: "I checked around with my society friends, and heard about a guy whose family has money—plenty of it. Name of Watterson."

"Last name or first?"

"That's the family name. Big in these parts."

"Means nothing to me."

"Well, Lloyd Watterson used to be a medical student. He's a big man, very strong—the kind of strength it might take to do some of the things the Butcher has done. And he has a history of mental disturbances."

"What kind of mental disturbances?"

"He's been going to psychiatrists since he was a school-boy."

"Do you know this guy?"

"Just barely. But I've heard things about him."

"Such as?"

"I hear he likes boys."

* * *

Lloyd Watterson lived in a two-story white house at the end of a dead-end street, a Victorian-looking miniature mansion among other such houses, where expansive lawns and towering hedges separated the world from the wealthy who lived within.

This wasn't the parental home, Vivian explained; Watterson lived here alone, apparently without servants. The grounds seemed well tended, though, and there was nothing about this house that said anyone capable of mass murder might live here. No blood spattered on the white porch; no body parts scattered about the lawn.

It was mid-afternoon, and I was having second thoughts.

"I don't even have a goddamn gun," I said.

"I do," she said, and showed me a little .25 automatic from her purse.

"Great. If he has a dog, maybe we can use that to scare it."

"This'll do the trick. Besides, a gun won't even be necessary. You're just here to talk."

The game plan was for me to approach Watterson as a cop, flashing my private detective's badge quickly enough to fool him (and that almost always worked), and question him, simply get a feel for whether or not he was a legitimate suspect, worthy of lobbying Eliot for action against. My say-so, Vivian felt, would be enough to get Eliot off the dime.

And helping Eliot bring the Butcher in would be a nice wedding present for my old friend; with his unstated but obvious political ambitions, the capture of the Kingsbury Run maniac would offset the damage his divorce had done him, in conservative, mostly Catholic Cleveland. He'd been the subject of near hero worship in the press here (Eliot was always good at getting press—Frank Nitti used to refer to him as "Eliot Press"); but the ongoing if sporadic slaughter of the

Butcher was a major embarrassment for Cleveland's fabled Safety Director.

So, leaving Vivian behind in the roadster (Watterson might recognize her), I walked up the curved sidewalk and went up on the porch and rang the bell. In the dark hardwood door there was opaque glass behind which I could barely make out movement, coming toward me.

The door opened, and a blond man about six-three with a baby-face and ice-blue eyes and shoulders that nearly filled the doorway looked out at me and grinned. A kid's grin, on one side of his face. He wore a polo shirt and short white pants; he seemed about to say, "Tennis anyone?"

But he said nothing, as a matter of fact; he just appraised me with those ice-blue, somewhat vacant eyes. I now knew how it felt for a woman to be ogled—which is to say, not necessarily good.

I said, "I'm an officer of the court," which in Illinois wasn't exactly a lie, and I flashed him my badge, but before I could say anything else, his hand reached out and grabbed the front of my shirt, yanked me inside and slammed the door.

He tossed me like a horseshoe, and I smacked into something—the stairway to the second floor, I guess; I don't know exactly—because I blacked out. The only thing I remember is the musty smell of the place.

I woke up minutes later, and found myself tied in a chair in a dank, dark room. Support beams loomed out of a packed dirt floor. The basement.

I strained at the ropes, but they were snug; not so snug as to cut off my circulation, but snug enough. I glanced around the room. I was alone. I couldn't see much—just a shovel against one cement wall. The only light came from a window off to my right, and there were hedges in front of the window, so the light was filtered.

Feet came tromping down the open wooden stairs. I saw his legs first, white as pastry dough. He was grinning. In his right hand was a cleaver. It shone, caught a glint of what little light there was.

"I'm no butcher," he said. His voice was soft, almost gentle. "Don't believe what you've heard. . ."

"Do you want to die?" I said.

"Of course not."

"Well then cut me loose. There's cops all over the place, and if you kill me, they'll shoot you down. You know what happens to cop killers, don't you?"

He thought that over, nodded.

Standing just to one side of me, displaying the cold polished steel of the cleaver, in which my face's frantic reflection looked back at me, he said, "I'm no butcher. This is a surgical tool. This is used for amputation, not butchery."

"Yeah. I can see that."

"I wondered when you people would come around."

"Do you want to be caught, Lloyd?"

"Of course not. I'm no different than you. I'm a public servant."

"How . . . how do you figure that, Lloyd?" My feet weren't tied to the chair; if he'd just step around in front of me . . .

"I only dispose of the flotsam. Not to mention jetsam."

"Not to mention that."

"Tramps. Whores. Weeding out the stock. Survival of the fittest. You know."

"That makes a lot of sense, Lloyd. But I'm not flotsam *or* jetsam. I'm a cop. You don't want to kill a cop. You don't want to kill a fellow public servant."

He thought about that.

"I think I have to, this time," he said.

He moved around the chair, stood in front of me, stroking

his chin, the cleaver gripped tight in his right hand, held about breastbone level.

"I *do* like you," Lloyd said, thoughtfully.

"And I like you, Lloyd," I said, and kicked him in the balls.

Harder than any man tied to a chair should be able to kick; but you'd be surprised what you can do, under extreme circumstances. And things rarely get more extreme than being tied to a chair with a guy with a cleaver coming at you.

Only he wasn't coming at me, now: now, he was doubled over, and I stood, the chair strapped to my back; managed, even so, to kick him in the face.

He tumbled back, gripping his groin, his head leaning back, stretching, tears streaming down his cheeks, cords in his neck taut; my shoe had caught him on the side of the face and broke the skin. Flecks of blood, like little red tears, spattered his cheeks, mingling with the real tears.

That's when the window shattered, and Vivian squeezed down in through; pretty legs first. And she gave me the little gun to hold on him while she untied me.

He was still on the dirt floor, moaning, when we went up the stairs and out into the sunny day, into a world that wasn't dank, onto earth that was grass-covered and didn't have God knows what buried under it.

We asked Eliot to meet us at his boathouse; we told him what had happened. He was livid; I never saw him angrier. But he held Vivian for a moment, and looked at her and said, "If anything had happened to you, I'd've killed you."

He poured all of us a drink; rum as usual. He handed me mine and said, "How could you get involved in something so harebrained?"

"I wanted to give my client something for his money," I said.

"You mean his daughter's killer."

"Why not?"

"I've been looking for the bastard three years, and you come to town and expect to find him in three days."

"Well, I did."

He smirked, shook his head. "I believe you did. But Watterson's family would bring in the highest-paid lawyers in the country and we'd be thrown out of court on our cans."

"What? The son of a bitch tried to cut me up with a cleaver!"

"Did he? Did he swing on you? Or did you enter his house under a false pretense, misrepresenting yourself as a law officer? And as far as that goes, *you* assaulted *him*. We have very little."

Vivian said, "You have the name of the Butcher."

Eliot nodded. "Probably. I'm going to make a phone call."

Eliot went into his den and came out fifteen minutes later.

"I spoke with Franklin Watterson, the father. He's agreed to submit his son for a lie detector test."

"To what end?"

"One step at a time," Eliot said.

Lloyd Watterson took the lie detector test twice—and on both instances denied committing the various Butcher slayings; his denials were, according to the machine, lies. The Watterson family attorney reminded Eliot that lie detector tests were not admissible as evidence. Eliot had a private discussion with Franklin Watterson.

Lloyd Watterson was committed, by his family, to an asylum for the insane. The Mad Butcher of Kingsbury Run— which to this day is marked "unsolved" in the Cleveland police records—did not strike again.

At least not directly.

Eliot married Evie MacMillan a few months after my

Cleveland visit, and their marriage was from the start disrupted by crank letters, postmarked from the same town as the asylum where Watterson had been committed. "Retribution will catch up with you one day," said one postcard, on the front of which was a drawing of an effeminate man grinning from behind prison bars. Mrs. Ness was especially unnerved by these continuing letters and cards.

Eliot's political fortunes waned, in the wake of the "unsolved" Butcher slayings. Known for his tough stance on traffic violators, he got mired in a scandal when one pre-dawn morning in March of 1942, his car skidded into an oncoming car on the West Shoreway. Eliot and his wife, and two friends, had been drinking. The police report didn't identify Eliot by name, but his license number—EN–1, well known to Cleveland citizens—was listed. And Eliot had left the scene of the accident.

Hit-and-run, the headlines said. Eliot's version was that his wife had been injured, and he'd raced her to a hospital—but not before stopping to check on the other driver, who confirmed this. The storm blew over, but the damage was done—Eliot's image in the Cleveland press was finally tarnished.

Two months later he resigned as Safety Director.

About that time, asylum inmate Lloyd Watterson managed to hang himself with a bed sheet, and the threatening mail stopped.

How much pressure those cards and letters put on the marriage I couldn't say; but in 1945 Eliot and Evie divorced, and Eliot married a third time a few months later. At the time he was serving as federal director of the program against venereal disease in the military. His attempt to run for Cleveland mayor in 1947 was a near disaster: Cleveland's one-time fair haired boy was a has-been with a hit-and-run scandal and two divorces and three marriages going against him.

He would not have another public success until the publication of his autobiographical book, *The Untouchables*—but that success was posthumous; he died shortly before it was published, never knowing that television and Robert Stack would give him lasting fame.

I saw Eliot, now and then, over the years; but I never saw Vivian again.

I asked him about her, once, when I was visiting him in Pennsylvania, in the early '50s. He told me she'd been killed in a boating accident in 1943.

"She's been dead for years, then," I said, the shock of it hitting me like a blow.

"That's right. But shed a tear for her, now, if you like. Tears and prayers can never come too late, Nate."

Amen, Eliot.

SCRAP

FRIDAY AFTERNOON, DECEMBER 8, 1939, I had a call from Jake Rubinstein to meet him at 3159 Roosevelt, which was in Lawndale, my old neighborhood. Jake was an all right guy, kind of talkative and something of a roughneck, but then on Maxwell Street, when I was growing up, developing a mouth and muscles was necessary for survival. I knew Jake had been existing out on the fringes of the rackets since then, but that was true of a lot of guys. I didn't hold it against him. I went into one of the rackets myself, after all—known in Chicago as the police department—and I figured Jake wouldn't hold that against me, either. Especially since I was private, now, and he wanted to hire me.

The afternoon was bitterly cold, snow on the ground but not snowing, as I sat parked in my sporty '32 Auburn across the street from the drugstore, over which was the union hall where Jake said to meet him. The Scrap Iron and Junk Handlers Union, he said. I didn't know there was one. They had unions for everything these days. My pop, an old union man, would've been pleased. I didn't much care.

I went up the flight of stairs and into the outer office; the meeting room was adjacent, at my left. The place was modest, like most union halls—if you're running a union you don't want the rank and file to think you're living it up—but the secretary behind the desk looked like a million. She was a brunette in a trim brown suit with big brown eyes and bright red lipstick. She'd soften the blow of paying dues any day.

She smiled at me and I forgot it was winter. "Would you be Mr. Heller?"

"I would. Would you be free for dinner?"

Her smile settled in one corner of her bright red mouth. "I wouldn't. Mr. Rubinstein is waiting for you in Mr. Martin's office."

And she pointed to the only door in the wall behind her, and I gave her a can't-blame-a-guy-for-trying look and went on in.

The inner office wasn't big but it seemed bigger than it was because it was underfurnished: just a clutter-free desk and a couple of chairs and two wooden file cabinets. Jake was sitting behind the desk, feet up on it, socks with clocks showing, as he read the Racing News.

"How are you, Jake," I said, and held out my hand.

He put the paper down, stood and grinned and shook my hand; he was a little guy, short I mean, but he had shoulders on him and his grip was a killer. He wore a natty dark blue suit and a red handpainted tie with a sunset on it and a hat that was a little big for him. He kept the hat on indoors—self-conscious about his thinning hair, I guess.

"You look good, Nate. Thanks for coming. Thanks for coming yourself and not sending one of your ops."

"Any excuse to get back to the old neighborhood, Jake," I said, pulling up a chair and sitting. "We're about four blocks from where my pop's bookshop was, you know."

"I know, I know," he said, sitting again. "What do you hear

from Barney these days?"

"Not much. When d'you get in the union racket, anyway? Last I heard you were a door-to-door salesman."

Jake shrugged. He had dark eyes and a weak chin and five o'clock shadow; make that six o'clock shadow. "A while ago," he allowed. "But it ain't really a racket. We're trying to give our guys a break."

I smirked at him. "In this town? Billy Skidmore isn't going to put up with a legit junk handlers' union."

Skidmore was a portly, dapperly dressed junk dealer and politician who controlled most of the major non-Capone gambling in town. Frank Nitti, Capone's heir, put up with that because Skidmore was also a bailbondsman, which made him a necessary evil.

"Skidmore's got troubles these days," Jake said. "He can't afford to push us around no more."

"You're talking about the income tax thing."

"Yeah. Just like Capone. He didn't pay his taxes and they got 'im for it."

"They indicted him, but that doesn't mean they got him. Anyway, where do I come in?"

Jake leaned forward, brow beetling. "You know a guy named Leon Cooke?"

"Can't say I do."

"He's a little younger than us, but he's from around here. He's a lawyer. He put this union together, two, three years ago. Well, about a year back he became head of an association of junkyard dealers, and the rank and file voted him out."

I shrugged. "Seems reasonable. In Chicago it wouldn't be *unusual* to represent both the employees *and* the employers, but kosher it ain't."

Jake was nodding. "Right. The new president is Johnny Martin. Know him?"

"Can't say I do."

"He's been with the Sanitary District for, oh, twenty or more years."

The Sanitary District controlled the sewage in the city's rivers and canals.

"He needed a hobby," I said, "so he ran for president of the junk handlers' union, huh?"

"He's a good man, Nate, he really is."

"What's your job?"

"I'm treasurer of the union."

"You're the collector, then."

"Well . . . yeah. Does it show?"

"I just didn't figure you for the accountant type."

He smiled sheepishly. "Every union needs a little muscle. Anyways, Cooke. He's trying to stir things up, we think. He isn't even legal counsel for the union anymore, but he's been coming to meetings, hanging around. We think he's been going around talking to the members."

"Got an election coming up?"

"Yeah. We want to know who he's talking to. We want to know if anybody's backing him."

"You think Nitti's people might be using him for a front?"

"Could be. Maybe even Skidmore. Playing both ends against the middle is Cooke's style. Anyways, can you shadow him and find out?"

"For fifteen a day and expenses, I can."

"Isn't that a little steep, Nate?"

"What's the monthly take on union dues around this joint?"

"Fifteen a day's fine," Jake said, shaking his head side to side, smiling.

"And expenses."

The door opened and the secretary came in, quickly, her silk stockings flashing.

"Mr. Rubinstein," she said, visibly upset, "Mr. Cooke is in the outer office. Demanding to see Mr. Martin."

"Shit," Jake said through his teeth. He glanced at me. "Let's get you out of here."

We followed the secretary into the outer office, where Cooke, a man of medium size in an off-the-rack brown suit, was pacing. A heavy topcoat was slung over his arm. In his late twenties, with thinning brown hair, Cooke was rather mild looking, with wire-rim glasses and cupid lips. Nonetheless, he was well and truly pissed off.

"Where's that bastard Martin?" he demanded of Jake. Not at all intimidated by the little strongarm man.

"He stepped out," Jake said.

"Then I'll wait. Till hell freezes over, if necessary."

Judging by the weather, that wouldn't be long.

"If you'll excuse us," Jake said, brushing by him. I followed.

"Who's this?" Cooke said, meaning me. "A new member of your goon squad? Isn't Fontana enough for you?"

Jake ignored that and I followed him down the steps to the street.

"He didn't mean Carlos Fontana, did he?" I asked.

Jake nodded. His breath was smoking, teeth chattering. He wasn't wearing a topcoat; we'd left too quickly for such niceties.

"Fontana's a pretty rough boy," I said.

"A lot of people who was in bootlegging," Jake said, shrugging, "had to go straight. What are you gonna do now?"

"I'll use the phone booth in the drugstore to get one of my ops out here to shadow Cooke. I'll keep watch till then. He got enough of a look at me that I don't dare shadow him myself."

Jake nodded. "I'm gonna go call Martin."

"And tell him to stay away?"

"That's up to him."

I shook my head. "Cooke seemed pretty mad."

"He's an asshole."

And Jake walked quickly down to a parked black Ford coupe, got in, and smoked off.

I called the office and told my secretary to send either Lou or Frankie out as soon as possible, whoever was available first; then I sat in the Auburn and waited.

Not five minutes later a heavyset, dark-haired man in a camel's hair topcoat went in and up the union-hall stairs. I had a hunch it was Martin. More than a hunch: he looked well and truly pissed off, too.

I could smell trouble.

I probably should have sat it out, but I got out of the Auburn and crossed Roosevelt and went up those stairs myself. The secretary was standing behind the desk. She was scared shitless. She looked about an inch away from crying.

Neither man was in the anteroom, but from behind the closed door came the sounds of loud voices.

"What's going on?" I said.

"That awful Mr. Cooke was in using Johnny . . . Mr. Martin's telephone, in his office, when Mr. Martin arrived."

They were scuffling in there, now.

"Any objection if I go in there and break that up?" I asked her.

"None at all," she said.

That was when we heard the shots.

Three of them, in rapid succession.

The secretary sucked in breath, covered her mouth, said, "My God . . . my God."

And I didn't have a gun, goddamnit.

I was still trying to figure out whether to go in there or not when the burly, dark-haired guy who I assumed (rightly) to be

Martin, still in the camel's hair topcoat, came out with a blue-steel revolver in his hand. Smoke was curling out of the barrel.

"Johnny, Johnny," the secretary said, going to him, clinging to him. "Are you all right?"

"Never better," he said, but his voice was shaking. He scowled over at me; he had bushy black eyebrows that made the scowl frightening. And the gun helped. "Who the hell are you?"

"Nate Heller. I'm a dick Jake Rubinstein hired to shadow Leon Cooke."

Martin nodded his head back toward the office. "Well, if you want to get started, he's on the floor in there."

I went into the office and Cooke was on his stomach; he wasn't dead yet. He had a bullet in the side; the other two slugs went through the heavy coat that had been slung over his arm.

"I had to do it," Martin said. "He jumped me. He attacked me."

"We better call an ambulance," I said.

"So, then, we can't just dump his body somewhere," Martin said, thoughtfully.

"I was hired to shadow this guy," I said. "It starts and ends there. You want something covered up, call a cop."

"How much money you got on you?" Martin said. He wasn't talking to me.

The secretary said, "Maybe a hundred."

"That'll hold us. Come on."

He led her through the office and opened a window behind his desk. In a very gentlemanly manner, he helped her out onto the fire escape.

And they were gone.

I helped Cooke onto his feet.

"You awake, pal?"

"Y-yes," he said. "Christ, it hurts."

"Mount Sinai Hospital's just a few blocks away," I said. "We're gonna get you there."

I wrapped the coat around him, to keep from getting blood on my car seat, and drove him to the hospital.

Half an hour later, I was waiting outside Cooke's room in the hospital hall when Captain Stege caught up with me.

Stege, a white-haired fireplug of a man with black-rimmed glasses and a pasty complexion—and that Chicago rarity, an honest cop—was not thrilled to see me.

"I'm getting sick of you turning up at shootings," he said.

"I do it just to irritate you. It makes your eyes twinkle."

"You left a crime scene."

"I hauled the victim to the hospital. I told the guy at the drugstore to call it in. Let's not get technical."

"Yeah," Stege grunted. "Let's not. What's your story?"

"The union secretary hired me to keep an eye on this guy Cooke. But Cooke walked in, while I was there, angry, and then Martin showed up, equally steamed."

I gave him the details.

As I was finishing up, a doctor came out of Cooke's room and Stege cornered him, flashing his badge.

"Can he talk, Doc?"

"Briefly. He's in critical condition."

"Is he gonna make it?"

"He should pull through. Stay only a few minutes, gentlemen."

Stege went in and I followed; I thought he might object, but he didn't.

Cooke looked pale, but alert. He was flat on his back. Stege introduced himself and asked for Cooke's story.

Cooke gave it, with lawyerlike formality: "I went to see Martin to protest his conduct of the union. I told Martin he ought to've obtained a pay raise for the men in one junkyard.

I told him our members were promised a pay increase, by a certain paper company, and instead got a wage cut—and that I understood he'd sided with the employer in the matter! He got very angry, at that, and in a little while we were scuffling. When he grabbed a gun out of his desk, I told him he was crazy, and started to leave. Then . . . then he shot me in the back."

Stege jotted that down, thanked Cooke and we stepped out into the hall.

"Think that was the truth?" Stege asked me.

"Maybe. But you really ought to hear Martin's side, too."

"Good idea, Heller. I didn't think of that. Of course, the fact that Martin lammed does complicate things, some."

"With all the heat on unions, lately, I can see why he lammed. There doesn't seem to be any doubt Martin pulled the trigger. But who attacked who remains in question."

Stege sighed. "You do have a point. I can understand Martin taking it on the lam, myself. He's already under indictment for another matter. He probably just panicked."

"Another matter?"

Stege nodded. "He and Terry Druggan and two others were indicted last August for conspiracy. Trying to conceal from revenue officers that Druggan was part owner of a brewery."

Druggan was a former bootlegger, a West Side hood who'd been loosely aligned with such non-Capone forces as the Bugs Moran gang. I was starting to think maybe my old man wouldn't have been so pleased by all this union activity.

"We'll stake out Martin's place," Stege said, "for all the good it'll do. He's got a bungalow over on Wolcott Avenue."

"Nice little neighborhood," I said.

"We're in the wrong racket," Stege admitted.

It was too late in the afternoon to bother going back to the office, now, so I stopped and had supper at Pete's Steaks and then headed back to my apartment at the Morrison Hotel. I

was reading a Westbrook Pegler column about what a bad boy
Willie Bioff was when the phone rang.

"Nate? It's Jake."

"Jake, I'm sorry I didn't call you or anything. I didn't have
any number for you but the union hall. You know about what
went down?"

"Do I. I'm calling from the Marquette station. They're
holding me for questioning."

"Hell, you weren't even there!"

"That's okay. I'm stalling 'em a little."

"Why, for Christ's sake?"

"Listen, Nate—we gotta hold this thing together. You gotta
talk to Martin."

"Why? How?"

"I'm gonna talk to Cooke. Cooke's the guy who hired me
to work for the union in the first place, and . . ."

"What? Cooke hired you?"

"Yeah, yeah. Look, I'll go see Cooke first thing in the
morning—that is, if you've seen Martin tonight, and worked
a story out. Something that'll make this all sound like an
accident . . ."

"I don't like being part of cover-ups."

"This ain't no fuckin' cover-up! It's business! Look, they
got the state's attorney's office in on this already. You know
who's taken over for Stege, already?"

"Tubbo Gilbert?"

"Himself," Jake said.

Captain Dan "Tubbo" Gilbert was the richest cop in Chicago. In the world. He was tied in with every mob, every fixer
in town.

"The local will be finished," Jake said. "He'll find something in the books and use that and the shooting as an excuse
to close the union down."

"Which'll freeze wages at current levels," I said. "Exactly what the likes of Billy Skidmore would want."

"Right. And then somebody else'll open the union back up, in six months or so. Somebody tied into the Nitti and Guzik crowd."

"As opposed to Druggan and Moran."

"Don't compare them to Nitti and Guzik. Those guys went straight, Nate."

"Please. I just ate. Moran got busted on a counterfeit railroad-bond scam just last week."

"Nobody's perfect. Nate, it's for the best. Think of your old man."

"Don't do that to me, Jake. I don't exactly think your union is what my pop had in mind when he was handing out pamphlets on Maxwell Street."

"Well, it's all that stands between the working stiffs and the Billy Skidmores."

"I take it you know where Martin is hiding out."

"Yeah. That secretary of his, her mother has a house in Hinsdale. Lemme give you the address . . ."

"Okay, Jake. It's against my better judgment, but okay . . ."

It took an hour to get there by car. Well after dark. Hinsdale was a quiet, well-fed little suburb, and the house at 409 Walnut Street was a two-story number in the midst of a healthy lawn. The kind of place the suburbs are full of, but which always seem shockingly sprawling to city boys like yours truly.

There were a few lights on, downstairs. I walked up onto the porch and knocked. I was unarmed. Probably not wise, but I was.

The secretary answered the door. Cracked it open.

She didn't recognize me at first.

"I'm here about our dinner date," I said.

Then, in relief, she smiled, opened the door wider.

"You're Mr. Heller."

"That's right. I never did get your name."

"Then how did you find me?"

"I had your address. I just didn't get your name."

"Well, it's Nancy. But what do you want, Mr. Heller?"

"Make it Nate. It's cold. Could I step in?"

She swallowed. "Sure."

I stepped inside; it was a nicely furnished home, but obviously the home of an older person: the doilies and ancient photo portraits were a dead giveaway.

"This is my mother's home," she said. "She's visiting relatives. I live here."

I doubted that; the commute would be impossible. If she didn't live with Martin, in his nifty little bungalow on South Wolcott, I'd eat every doilie in the joint.

"I know that John Martin is here," I said. "Jake Rubinstein told me. He asked me to stop by."

She didn't know what to say to that.

Martin stepped out from a darkened doorway into the living room. He was in rolled-up shirt sleeves and no tie. He looked frazzled. He had the gun in his hand.

"What do you want?" he said. His tone was not at all friendly.

"You're making too big a deal out of this," I said. "There's no reason to go on the lam. This is just another union shooting—the papers're full of 'em."

"I don't shoot a man every day," Martin said.

"I'm relieved to hear that. How about putting the heater away, then?"

Martin sneered and tossed the piece on a nearby floral couch. He was a nasty man to have a nice girl like this. But then, so often nice girls do like nasty men.

I took it upon myself to sit down. Not on the couch: on a chair, with a soft seat and curved wooden arms.

Speaking of curves, Nancy, who was wearing a blue print dress, was standing wringing her hands, looking about to cry.

"I could use something to drink," I said, wanting to give her something to do.

"Me too," Martin said. "Beer. For him, too."

"Beer would be fine," I said, magnanimously.

She went into the kitchen.

"What's Jake's idea?" Martin asked.

I explained that Jake was afraid the union would be steamrolled by crooked cops and political fixers, should this shooting blow into something major, first in the papers, then in the courts.

"Jake wants you to mend fences with Cooke. Put together some story you can both live with. Then find some way you can run the union together, or pay him off or something."

"Fuck that shit!" Martin said. He stood up. "What's wrong with that little kike, has he lost his marbles?"

"A guy who works on the west side," I said, "really ought to watch his goddamn mouth where the Jew-baiting's concerned."

"What's it to you? You're Irish."

"Does Heller sound Irish to you? Don't let the red hair fool you."

"Well fuck you, too, then. Cooke's a lying little kike, and Jake's still in bed with him. Damn! I thought I could trust that little bastard . . ."

"I think you can. I think he's trying to hold your union together, with spit and rubber bands. I don't know if it's worth holding together. I don't know what you're in it for—maybe you really care about your members, a little. Maybe it's the money. But if I were you, I'd do some fast thinking, put together a story you can live with and let Jake try to sell it to Cooke. Then when the dust settles you'll still have a piece of the action."

Martin walked over and pointed a thick finger at me. "I don't believe you, you slick son of a bitch. I think this is a set-up. Put together to get me to come in, give myself up and go straight to the lock-up, while Jake and Cooke tuck the union in their fuckin' belt!"

I stood. "That's up to you. I was hired to deliver a message. I delivered it. Now if you'll excuse me."

He thumped his finger in my chest. "You tell that little kike Rubinstein for me that . . ."

I smacked him.

He don't go down, but it backed him up. He stood there looking like a confused bear and then growled and lumbered at me with massive fists out in front, ready to do damage.

So I smacked the bastard again, and again. He went down that time. I helped him up. He swung clumsily at me, so I hit him in the side of the face and he went down again. Stayed down.

Nancy came in, a glass of beer in either hand, and said, "What . . . ?" Her brown eyes wide.

"Thanks," I said, taking one glass, chugging it. I wiped the foam off my face with the back of a hand and said, "I needed that."

And I left them there.

The next morning, early, while I was still at the Morrison, shaving in fact, the phone rang.

It was Jake.

"How did it go last night?" he asked.

I told him.

"Shit," he said. "I'll still talk to Cooke, though. See if I can't cool this down some."

"I think it's too late for that."

"Me too," Jake said glumly.

Martin came in on Saturday; gave himself up to Tubbo Gilbert. Stege was off the case. The story Martin told was considerably different from Cooke's: he said Cooke was in the office using the phone ("Which he had no right to do!") and Martin told him to leave; Cooke started pushing Martin around, and when Martin fought back, Cooke drew a gun. Cooke (according to Martin) hit him over the head with it and knocked him down. Then Cooke supposedly hit him with the gun again and Martin got up and they struggled and the gun went off. Three times.

The gun was never recovered. If it was really Cooke's gun, of course, it would have been to Martin's advantage to produce it; but he didn't.

Martin's claim that Cooke attacked and beat him was backed up by the fact that his face was badly bruised and battered. So I guess I did him a favor, beating the shit out of him.

Martin was placed under bond on a charge of intent to kill. Captain Dan "Tubbo" Gilbert, representing the state's attorney's office, confiscated the charter of the union, announcing that it had been run "purely as a racket." Shutting it down until such time that "the actual working members of the union care to continue it, and elect their own officers."

That sounded good in the papers, but in reality it meant Skidmore and company had been served.

I talked to Stege about it, later, over coffee and bagels in the Dill Pickle Deli below my office on Van Buren.

"Tubbo was telling the truth about the union being strictly a racket," Stege said. "They had a thousand members paying two bucks a head a month. Legitimate uses counted for only seven hundred bucks' worth a month. Martin's salary, for example, was only a hundred-twenty bucks."

"Well he's shit out of luck, now," I said.

"He's still got his position at the Sanitary District," Stege said. "Of course, he's got to beat the rap for the assault-to-kill charge, first . . ." Stege smiled at the thought. "And Mr. Cooke tells a more convincing story than Martin does."

The trouble was, Cooke never got to tell it, not in court. He took a sudden turn for the worse, as so many people in those days did in Chicago hospitals, when they were about to testify in a major trial. Cooke died on the first Friday of January, 1940. There was no autopsy. His last visitor, I was told, was Jake Rubinstein.

When the union was finally re-opened, however, Jake was no longer treasurer. He was still involved in the rackets, though, selling punchboards, working for Ben "Zuckie the Bookie" Zuckerman, with a short time out for a wartime stint in the air force. He went to Dallas, I've heard, as representative of Chicago mob interests there, winding up running some strip joints. Rumor has it he was involved in other cover-ups, over the years.

By that time, of course, Jake was better known as Jack.

And he'd shortened his last name to Ruby.

I Owe Them One

My friend and research associate George Hagenauer provided his usual support system on all of these stories, but he was particularly helpful on the novella, "Dying in the Post-War World." Among other things, he did hours of newspaper research, took me on a walking tour of the various crime scenes, and developed the background for the character Otto Bergstrum.

"Dying in the Post-War World" is based on a real case, but (with the exception of Bill Drury and a few minor police officials), the characters in the story are wholly fictional and are not intended to be representations of their real-life counterparts or anyone else. The time frame of the story differs somewhat from that of the real crimes, and the aspect of the story involving Sam Giancana (a real historical figure, obviously) is a fanciful one. My "solution" to this famous case is equally fanciful. However, like Nate Heller, I have come to the conclusion that it is unlikely William Heirens—the real-life convicted Lipstick Killer—was truly guilty of the kidnapping and murder of young Susan Degnan. (George Hagenauer has serious doubts that Heirens was guilty of any of the murders.)

I would like to acknowledge as source material for the novella the following books: *The Don* (1977), William Brashler; *Murders Sane and Mad* (1965), Miriam Allen deFord; *Murder Man* (1984), Thomas Downs; *"Before I Kill More . . ."* (1955), Lucy Freeman; *Mafia Princess* (1984), Antoinette Giancana and Thomas C. Renner; and *Wartime Racketeers* (1945), Harry Lever and Joseph Young. Also, the article "Kill-Crazed Animal?" by Robert McClory, which appeared in the Chicago *Reader* (August 25, 1989).

I would like to acknowledge the source material for the short stories in this book, as well. Incidentally, several of these stories (including "Private Consultation" and "Marble Mildred") seriously suggest solutions for crimes long clouded in doubt and controversy.

"Private Consultation" derives in part from "The Wynekoop Case" by Craig Rice (1947), as reprinted in *The Chicago Crime Book,* 1967; "Who Killed Rheta Wynekoop?" by Harry Read, *Real Detective Magazine,* April 1934; and "The Justice Story," a 1987 New York *Daily News* column by Joseph McNamara.

"House Call" is indebted to the article "The Peacock Case" by LeRoy F. McHugh (who was, incidentally, the basis for "McCue" in Hecht and MacArthur's *Front Page*) in *Chicago Murders,* "Joseph Bolton, the Almost Indestructible Husband" by Nellise Child. Also helpful was the Mildred Bolton entry in *Look for the Woman* (1981) by Jay Robert Nash.

"The Strawberry Teardrop" is indebted to two non-fiction books, *Four Against the Mob* by Oscar Fraley (1961) and *Cleveland—The Best Kept Secret* by George E. Condon (1967). I explore the Mad Butcher of Kingsbury Run case in more detail in the novel *Butcher's Dozen* (Bantam Books, 1988), an expansion of this short story, based upon further research at Western Reserve Historical Society in Cleveland; however,

Nate Heller does not appear in the novel-length version.

"Scrap" is primarily based upon newspaper research, although I should also acknowledge *Maxwell Street* (1977) by Ira Berkow; and *The Plot to Kill the President* (1981) by G. Robert Blakey and Richard N. Billings.

I wish to thank Robert Randisi, who—as editor of the semi-annual Private Eye Writers of America anthologies—first published four of these stories; thanks also to Otto Penzler and Bill Malloy, both of Mysterious Press. And I'd like to thank Ed Gorman, editor of *The Black Lizard Anthology of Crime Fiction* (1987), who commissioned "Scrap" and wrote the introduction to this volume.

The usual, but no less sincere, thanks to my agent Dominick Abel; and a big tip of the fedora to Louis Wilder and Lou Kannenstine of Foul Play Press, both of whom are a pleasure to work with. Thanks also to my friends Miguel Ferrer and Ed Neumier, who both made valuable suggestions about the novella "Dying in the Post-War World."

These stories could not have been written without the love, encouragement and support of my wife—Nate's mother—Barbara Collins.